W9-AZG-548

INSTRUCTIONS

Kevin Bolger

Illustrated by Aaron Blecha

razOr
bill

An Imprint of Penguin Group (USA) Inc.

Zombiekins

RAZORBILL

Published by the Penguin Group
Penguin Young Readers Group
345 Hudson Street, New York, New York 10014, U.S.A.
Penguin Group (USA) Inc., 375 Hudson Street, New York, New York 10014, U.S.A.
Penguin Group (Canada), 90 Eglinton Avenue East, Suite 700, Toronto, Ontario,
Canada M4P 2Y3 (a division of Pearson Penguin Canada Inc.)
Penguin Books Ltd, 80 Strand, London WC2R 0RL, England
Penguin Ireland, 25 St Stephen's Green, Dublin 2, Ireland
(a division of Penguin Books Ltd)
Penguin Group (Australia), 250 Camberwell Road, Camberwell,
Victoria 3124, Australia
(a division of Pearson Australia Group Pty Ltd)
Penguin Books India Pvt Ltd, 11 Community Centre, Panchsheel Park,
New Delhi – 110 017, India
Penguin Group (NZ), 67 Apollo Drive, Mairangi Bay, Auckland 1311, New Zealand
(a division of Pearson New Zealand Ltd)
Penguin Books (South Africa) (Pty) Ltd, 24 Sturdee Avenue, Rosebank,
Johannesburg 2196, South Africa

Penguin Books Ltd, Registered Offices: 80 Strand, London WC2R 0RL, England

10 9 8 7 6 5 4 3 2 1

Library of Congress Cataloging-in-Publication Data is available

ISBN: 978-1-59514-367-9

Printed in the United States of America

This one's for you, Mom.
—K. B.

For Nicky, my zombie bride
—A. B.

THE LITTLE TOWN OF DEMENTEDYVILLE WAS A TIDY, uneventful town. The sort of place where home owners took care never to let their well-tended lawns become overrun by unsightly weeds or children, and birds sang in all the trees—but only between the hours of nine and five, as per the town's bylaws.

But even in Dementedyville there was one house that stood out from all the others....

Number 4 Shadow Lane, the Widow Imavitch's place, was so spooky that children dared one another to go trick-or-treating to the door each Halloween. But nobody ever did. Naturally everyone believed the place was haunted. And then, of course, there were the strange stories about the Widow herself....

Most of these rumors were started by Reuben Rumpelfink, the Widow's neighbor. He was always complaining about her eccentric ways: About the

weeds that grew wild in her garden, which he claimed had tried to eat his dog. About the bonfire parties she held whenever there was a full moon, where her guests (disreputable characters of questionable grooming habits) carried on loudly from midnight to sunrise. And about the mysterious storm cloud that hung over her yard in every kind of weather.

"That woman is a freak!" Mr. Rumpelfink told anyone who would listen. "She's a danger to us all!"

The day this story begins, Mr. Rumpelfink was leading a frenzied mob of townspeople up Shadow Lane, heading straight for the Widow's gates. Some of the crowd carried pitchforks, or axes, or flaming torches. Their faces were set in looks of fierce determination, as if they had some grim purpose in mind and would let nothing stand in their way....

News of a sale had spread all over town in minutes. People dropped whatever they were doing and rushed right over. Nobody wanted to miss out on any deals.

As the bargain-crazed mob surged toward the Widow's laneway, the gates suddenly swung open, *as if by magic....*

"Probably just motion sensors," Miranda told her friend Stanley Nudelman. "Why do you always have to go imagining things?"

Stanley and Miranda walked home this way from school every day.

"Let's go take a look," Miranda said. "I bet the Widow has lots of cool stuff."

"I'm not sure that's such a good idea," Stanley hesitated. "You know what people say about her...."

"Don't tell me you actually believe all those dumb rumors?" Miranda scoffed. "Come on, Stanley. Just because somebody lives in a spooky old house, and wears black all the time, and has a toad for a pet, and keeps a broomstick chained to a bicycle rack by her door, and talks to bats, and appears and disappears mysteriously wherever a certain black cat is around, *that doesn't make her a witch.*"

But Stanley was not the kind of boy who liked taking chances.

"I don't know...." he fretted.

"Oh, come on," Miranda said. "What's the worst thing that could happen?"

ONCE STANLEY AND
Miranda were inside
the gates, the Widow's
sale was a big disappoint-
ment. There was noth-
ing particularly strange or
mysterious about the items
she was selling. It was just
a bunch of kitchen

stuff, old clothes, puzzles that were missing
pieces, a cracked wardrobe mirror,
some dusty old furniture—the
same junk you always find at
yard sales. Except the Widow's
mirror had a ghost in it and all
her chairs bit.

13

The Widow herself was nowhere in sight, but her cat seemed to be following them. It kept winding in and out of their legs, purring.

Miranda crouched down to pet it. But Stanley just said "Nice kitty" without getting too close because he was allergic.

Mr. Rumpelfink was there too, hunched over a pad of paper, scribbling furtive notes as he moved from table to table inspecting the items for sale.

"I wonder what *he's* doing here?" Stanley said.

"Snooping, probably," Miranda guessed. "I bet he's trying to find something he can use against the Widow.

"Hey, speaking of Mr. Rumpelfink," said Miranda, "doesn't this pincushion look just like him?"

She held up a homemade doll with shiny silver pins stuck into it. It really did look a lot like Mr. Rumpelfink. Miranda turned the doll over in her hands, pulling the pins in and out, in and out.

"Weird," Stanley agreed. But something else had caught his eye....

It was some sort of stuffed animal, still in its box. Only it wasn't like any stuffed animal Stanley had ever seen before....

It had one floppy bunny ear on a teddy bear's head and body...webbed paws with sharp claws... feet like a lizard...and two fangs instead of a rabbit's buckteeth.

Its eyes were sewn on like buttons—one fixed straight ahead with a cold, blank stare, the other dangling on a loose thread. Its fur was mangled and matted. And even still in the box, it was covered in cobwebs.

Something about the strange toy appealed to Stanley. It was so different from his kid sister's annoying stuffed animals, with their treacly songs and their adorable remarks whenever you squeezed their tummies.

"Check this out," Stanley said, showing Miranda. "I think I might buy it."

"Purrr-fect," mewled a voice. It was Mrs. Imavitch. She must've been standing behind them all along— how could they not have noticed her? "Zat is a *most* remarkable toy."

"Y-yeah, it's, uh, pretty freaky...." Stanley said, a little rattled by her popping up out of nowhere. "I bet everyone at school would think it's cool."

"Ah, yes, that could cause *qvuite* a sensation," the Widow said mysteriously. "It might give your schoolmates a bit of excitement some of zem vould never forget—*and some vould never remember....*"

"Huh?" Stanley asked. She was starting to creep him out a little. "W-what do you mean?"

"My dear, zat is no ordinary toy," the Widow started to explain. "It's—"

But then, noticing Mr. Rumpelfink eavesdropping on them from behind a rack of black and off-black robes, she paused mid-sentence.

"...*full of surprises*," the Widow said at last, with a very speaking look. Then she whispered, "*Just be sure to read zee instructionz.*"

"Vait here," the Widow added, then disappeared in the direction of her house.

"Boy, no wonder people think she's weird," Miranda said. "What do you think *that* was all about?"

"I don't know," Stanley said, suddenly having second thoughts about his new toy. "Do you think maybe it's cursed or something?"

Miranda just rolled her eyes.

"Stanley, for the hundredth time, there's no such thing as curses and witches and all that silly voodoo stuff," she said, flinging the pincushion back onto the table.

A minute later, Mrs. Imavitch returned with a bag of leftover Halloween candy— taffy, the kind no one liked, wrapped in waxed paper covered with silhouettes

18

of vampire bats and witches on broomsticks.

Stanley tried to politely turn down the wretched candy, but the Widow kept pressing it on him.

"Take it," she urged, with more strange looks. "You never know when it might come in handy. I never get any trick-or-treaters at my place anyvay," the Widow added. "I guess kids today just aren't into Halloween like zey vere in my day."

Stanley took the taffy and paid for Zombiekins. By now he just wanted to get out of there. But even as he was leaving with Miranda, the Widow called after him one last time, "*Don't forget to read zee instructionz!*"

3

BUT OF COURSE STANLEY NEVER DID READ THE
instructions. He took Zombiekins out
of its box and threw the packaging in a trashcan before
he reached the end
of the block.
But he kept the
taffy in his knap-
sack because
he was afraid to
offend the Widow by

throwing it out. Miranda said he was crazy to think she'd ever know, but there was something mysterious about the Widow, and Stanley was not the kind of boy who liked taking chances.

Stanley walked up the lane to his house wondering, what was so special about his new toy. What had the Widow been trying to tell him?

The sound of the front door opening brought Stanley's dog Fetch barking from the far end of the house. Fetch came bounding around the corner to

meet Stanley with his tail wagging his whole body like a rubber noodle.

But when Fetch saw what Stanley was holding he skidded to a halt, knocking a potted geranium off an end table. His tail drooped between his legs. He started yelping and backpedaling wildly, knocking over the end table, then disappeared back around the corner as quickly as he'd come.

"Some watchdog," Stanley chuckled.

"*Stanley, dear,*" his mother called from the kitchen, "*can you check on your sister?*"

Stanley found his two-year-old sister Rosalie in the TV room. She was dressed in her princess costume and busy building a wobbly castle out of the good china, a pair of crystal vases, her mother's wedding dress, open paint cans, sharp objects, broken glass, a box marked FIREWORKS, and miscellaneous electrical hazards.

"*It's okay, Mom,*" Stanley called back reassuringly. "*She's in here.*"

"Hi, Stanley," Baby Rosalie said. "What you got? I see it?"

She grabbed Zombiekins out of Stanley's hands

before he could answer. There was a low growl from under the couch where Fetch had taken cover.

"Ooo, him *scary*," Rosalie said.

"Yeah, well, it's sort of a 'zombie' stuffed animal," Stanley explained.

"'Zombie'?" Rosalie said. "Why him 'zombie'?"

Uh-oh. How was Stanley going to answer that one? He didn't want to scare her. But, on the other hand, he didn't believe in sheltering her from the facts of life, either.

"Well, a zombie is a reanimated corpse that's been revivified by witchcraft or transformed by the bite of another zombie," Stanley explained.

Rosalie stared back at him blankly.

"But don't worry," Stanley added, "this isn't a *real* zombie. It's just a stuffy with a sort of macabre, half-dead appearance."

"Oh," she replied.

She gave Zombiekins a long, thoughtful look.

"Him still scary," she concluded at last.

AN HOUR LATER, STANLEY WAS IN THE MIDDLE OF
doing his homework when Fetch appeared in his
bedroom doorway, barking at him.

"Not now, Fetch," Stanley said. "I'm too busy
doing homework to play with you."

"Woof!" Fetch barked again, more urgently. "Woof! Woof!"

Most people assumed Fetch was dumb just because he was always doing things like licking frozen fire hydrants and peeing on the rug. But Stanley knew Fetch was smarter than everybody thought. If only his family had named him Fido or Spot, maybe he wouldn't have flunked out of obedience school and things might've been different. As it was, no wonder the poor dog had been confused with everybody yelling "Sit, Fetch!" and "Stay, Fetch!" and "No, Fetch—NOT ON THE TEACHER'S SHOE!!!" at him all the time.

Fetch barked again, then pointed with his paw down the hall. For some reason, Stanley got the feeling Fetch was trying to tell him something.

"What is it, boy?" Stanley asked. "Are you trying to tell me something?"

Fetch put his front paws to his throat and rolled on the ground like he was choking himself. Then he stood on his hind legs and walked with his front paws stretched out before him like Frankenstein. Then he pointed down the hall again.

Fetch *was* trying to tell him something—Stanley was almost sure of it.

"What is it, boy?" Stanley asked again

Fetch sighed and rolled his eyes. Even Lassie's family was never *this* thick. Finally the dog gave up and took Stanley's hand in his mouth.

"Do you want me to follow you?" Stanley asked as Fetch dragged him out into the hall. "Is that it, boy?"

Fetch led Stanley down the hall and stopped outside the playroom door. Stanley could hear strange noises coming from the other side—a sort of strangled gurgling sound. . . .

Slowly, he turned the knob . . . pushed the door open . . . and . . .

SOMETHING JUMPED OUT AT HIM!!!

It had dead sunken eyes—gray rotting flesh—blood dripping from a mouth full of fangs—a pink sequined dress with matching tiara—

Stanley jumped back. Fetch yelped and peed on the carpet.

"Look, Stanley," the ghoulish apparition said, "I a zombie princess!"

It was Baby Rosalie, wearing an old rubber Halloween mask with her princess outfit.

"I having a tea party!" she said. Then, with a strangled gurgling sound, she pretended to sip tea from an empty teacup.

Seated at a doll's tea table on the playroom floor was Zombiekins. Across the table was Whimsy the Pfoo, a teddy of his sister's that went around wearing nothing but a sweater.

"Hugs are cuddle-wonderful," Whimsy announced. "Have a huggsy-wuggsy day...."

Zombiekins just sat there silently, one eye fixed straight ahead and the other hanging loosely by a thread.

Stanley looked at Fetch. Maybe his dog *was* pretty dumb after all. He turned to go back to his room— and suddenly felt something warm and wet soaking through his sock...:

THAT NIGHT, WHILE STANLEY AND HIS FAMILY WERE sleeping in their beds, something strange and unexpected happened in the playroom....

The room was dark and eerily quiet. Nothing stirred but a curtain that shivered now and then in a cold night draft. In the deep midnight stillness, the ticking of a clock down the hall seemed to echo like a banging gavel through the upstairs rooms. (And it was a digital clock.) A full moon shone in through the window, and as it rose in the sky, hour by hour, a shaft of moonlight crept slowly across the floor. . . .

Until in the deepest, darkest part of the night, its moonglow shone at last on a heap of toys in a corner. . . .

Something stirred in the depths of the pile. Suddenly the toys at the top were pushed aside. . . . And something . . . began to emerge . . . from underneath. . . .

Somewhere, a scream of terror ripped through the night. . . .

(Not in this story, mind you, but *somewhere*.)

And then, from under the pile of toys, Zombiekins slowly arose. One eye was fixed straight ahead in a cold blank stare, the other lolled sidelong toward the floor. A strange voice rang out in the dark:

"*Oooo, I feel huggily-snuggily.*"

It was Whimsy, still sitting on his frumpy rump at the tidy tea table.

Zombiekins started to cross the room, walking stiffly and with a limp—one leg swiveling on its teddy-bear joint, the other dragging like a dead limb….

Stump!—scri-i-i-i-i-itch … **Stump!—scri-i-i-i-i-itch** … **Stump!—scri-i-i-i-i-itch** …

Slowly and steadily, Zombiekins advanced across the playroom, driven by some dark, unknown purpose.

"A hug a day keeps the frownies away…." Whimsy enthused.

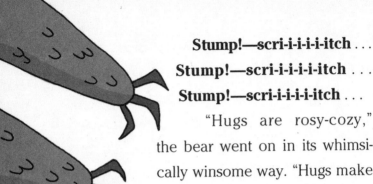

Stump!—scri-i-i-i-i-itch . . .
Stump!—scri-i-i-i-i-itch . . .
Stump!—scri-i-i-i-i-itch . . .

"Hugs are rosy-cozy," the bear went on in its whimsically winsome way. "Hugs make me feel fuzzy-wuzzy in my —GLAAAWWWRRKKK!!!!"

A moment later, Whimsy lay silenced on his side. Fluffy stuffy guts spilled from a slashy gash in his rum-tum-tummy, oozing onto the floor in a sorry-gory mess.

Elsewhere in the playroom, another toy broke into an inappropriately cheery song:

"Floating along on a birthday cake
Upon a raspberry-soda-pop lake . . .

Surrounded by choco-late sundae mountains,
Candy-cane rainbows and butterscotch fountains . . . "

It was Benny the Singing Dinosaur. Zombiekins turned and began walking stiffly toward the source of the music.

"We'll merry-go-round the dreamy day long. . . ." Benny sang.

Stump!—scri-i-i-i-i-itch . . .

"Singing our birthday-cake rowboat songs!"

Stump!—scri-i-i-i-i-itch . . .

"Go for a swim with the iddle-bitty fishes . . ."

   Stump!—scri-i-i-i-i-itch . . .

"Tickling our toesies like Mummy's kisses—"

There was a loud shower of sparks, and a severed dino head rolled away into a corner, where it went on singing like a broken record:

> "*Swim with the—fishes ... Swim with the*
> *—fishes ... Swim with the—fishes ...*"

Zombiekins turned toward another corner of the playroom....

"Schlemmo wants up," whimpered a furry orange toy far too adorable to be called a monster. Its voice was high-pitched and tinny, like some pre-adolescent chipmunk. "Up, up ... Schlemmo wants up!"

Zombiekins started walking, stiffly and with a

limp, one leg dragging like a dead limb....

Stump!—scri-i-i-i-i-itch ...

"Schlemmo doesn't want to play right now," the cute and cuddly monster simpered.

Stump!—scri-i-i-i-i-itch ...

"Up, up! Schlemmo wants up-up!" the toy too adorable to be called a monster begged in its tinny-tiny voice. But there was nobody to hear.

Stump!—scri-i-i-i-i-itch ...

"...Schlemmo wants...Schlemmo doesn't—"

THE NEXT MORNING, STANLEY WAS YANKED OUT
of sleep bright and early by an alarm clock with no
snooze button—the cold wet nose of his dog Fetch.

"Nghhhh!" Stanley grumbled, rolling over. "Go
away.... Sleeping..."

But Fetch just climbed halfway onto Stanley's
bed, barking and licking Stanley's face.

"Bad dog!" Stanley drowsily protested. "Go!"

Fetch barked again and pointed out into the hall.

"Unghhh," Stanley groaned, wiping sleep from his eyes and dog slobber from his face. "Not *this* again."

Moments later, Fetch was dragging Stanley down the hall to the playroom once more. Stanley wasn't prepared for the grisly scene of toy-room tragedy he found there.

The floor was strewn with bits of savaged stuffies: Teddy bears with the stuffing ripped out of them … Decapitated dinos … A dismembered Schlemmo …

Stanley just stood in the doorway, speechless. At first he was too stunned to understand what had happened. Then it started to sink in.

"Bad, Fetch!" Stanley scolded.

Boy, that dog had really done it this time. When Stanley's mom found out about this, she was going to send Fetch to a farm for sure, like she was always threatening.

Stanley gave Fetch a dirty look. But instead of drooping his ears and tucking his tail between his legs in heartfelt canine remorse, the dumb dog just barked again and pointed to Zombiekins sitting unharmed in the middle of the crime scene.

Well, Stanley thought with relief, at least *his* toy had been spared. He took Zombiekins and put it in his school bag by the front door.

Then he went back to the playroom, gathered the remains of the other stuffies into a box, and hid them under his bed before he left for school. He didn't want Fetch to get sent to a farm. After all, the poor dog couldn't help it if he was born stupid.

AT SCHOOL, ZOMBIEKINS WAS EVEN MORE OF A HIT than Stanley could have hoped. Kids from all over the playground stopped whatever they were doing to crowd around him for a look at his weird, one-of-a-kind toy. Girls dropped their skipping ropes. Boys paused in the middle of pummeling each other. One kid wandered off the school grounds blindfolded when the friends he was playing blindfold tag with rushed away without telling him.

"Cool!" exclaimed Kathleen.

"Freaky!" complimented Fiona.

"Ew, gross!" squealed Butch.

"If you come anywhere near me with that thing," shrieked Big Tony, "I'll *scream!*"

But then a growl from the back of the crowd silenced all the others:

"Nice *doll*, Nudelman."

It was Knuckles Bruzkowski, the school bully.

The crowd around Stanley split up as quickly as it had formed. Girls hopscotched it out of there. Boys suddenly recalled they had people to punch at the other end of the yard. Somebody remembered the

kid who was "it" in blindfold tag and went to retrieve him from traffic.

Knuckles was the terror of every kid in Dementedyville Elementary, but he always reserved a special place in his hurt for Stanley. He never saw Stanley without giving him a sucker punch, wedgie, or purple nurple—so when Stanley could help it, Knuckles never saw him at all.

But this time Stanley had let his guard down, and before he could duck for cover under the play structure, tunnel though the sand to safety, run home and transfer to another school, Knuckles grabbed hold of him.

And the next thing Stanley knew, he was dangling upside down in the chains of the tire swing and Knuckles was clenching Zombiekins in one of his meaty fists.

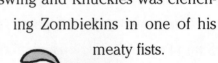

"Why are its eyes like that?" Knuckles grunted, holding the strange stuffy away from him as if he wasn't sure what to make of it.

"I-I got it at Mrs. Imavitch's yard sale," Stanley stammered.

Knuckles' eyes widened.

"You got this from *the Widow*?" he said. Stanley would've almost said he looked afraid.

The bell rang. All over the school ground, children stopped laughing and playing and trudged into line like condemned prisoners. Stanley felt a wave of panic, remembering the time Knuckles hung him from the basketball net at first recess on a rainy day and he wasn't discovered until home time. (His teeth still chattered just thinking about it.)

"Hey," said a voice behind them. "Give that back to Stanley right now!"

It was Miranda, of course. She was the only kid in school who ever dared stand up to Knuckles.

Knuckles' lips curled in a snarl, but he didn't make a move toward her.

Instead he just wrenched the swing tighter around Stanley.

"*Make me*," Knuckles growled.

"We're not afraid of you, Duane," Miranda said.

Knuckles' eyes flashed with anger at the mention of his given name. He cranked the swing another couple notches.

"Yes, we are!" Stanley squeaked.

Fortunately, at that moment, the duty teacher Mrs. Plumdotty saw them from across the yard.

"*Stan*-ley," she called from the back door, where she was herding kids into the school. "Stop playing on those swings and line up. You heard the bell, dear."

"Yeah, Stanley, dear," Knuckles snorted. He gave Zombiekins one last, uncertain look and stuffed it into the space where the chain made a collar around Stanley's neck. Then he wound the swing a couple notches tighter and released it with a spin.

"*Catch you later*, Nudelman," Knuckles growled as he lumbered away.

8

ALL THE WAY UP TO THEIR CLASS ON THE THIRD floor, Stanley had to listen to Miranda lecture him for the hundredth time about standing up to Knuckles. She had this theory that Knuckles would leave Stanley alone if only he would stick up for himself. Stanley had his own theory—that whenever Miranda did stick up for him, it only made Knuckles' poundings worse.

Halfway up the last flight of stairs, they were startled by a voice from above.

"*Mister* Nudelman ..."

Their teacher Mr. Baldengrumpy was standing at the top of the stairwell with a look on his face like he'd just bitten into a pickled lemon.

Stanley froze. It was never good when a teacher called you "Mister."

"Did you *really* expect to get away with it this time?" Mr. Baldengrumpy croaked.

It didn't take Stanley long to guess what his teacher was cross about. Mr. Baldengrumpy was obsessed with walking properly in lines. He made the class practice fire drills three times a week. Three times a week he marched them up and down the halls, teaching them to be quiet by yelling at them. He said they had to learn to exit the building in a slow and orderly manner in case there was ever a real fire. If there was ever a real fire, he wanted to be sure his class could exit the slowest.

One of Mr. Baldengrumpy's rules was that they had to walk up the stairs on the left, down on the right. Stanley didn't mean to be a troublemaker, but he was always forgetting.

"Well, you can just march back down there and come up again on the right side," Mr. Baldengrumpy barked.

"Er, but I thought you said we were supposed to come up on the *left*?" Stanley meekly replied.

"*Don't get smart with me, young man!*" Mr. Baldengrumpy fumed.

So Stanley trudged all the way back down the stairs and came up again on the right side, which is to say, the left.

In class, Stanley was in trouble again before he could even take his book out for the first lesson. He was just minding his own business while the rest of the class copied out some spelling words when for no reason at all Felicity Lickspittle piped up from the desk in front of him, "Mr. Baldengrumpy, Stanley has a *toy* in his desk."

Mr. Baldengrumpy stopped writing on the chalkboard and glared down at Stanley, whose first reflex was naturally to shove Zombiekins deeper into his desk. But that only made his teacher more cross.

Stanley handed Zombiekins over and Mr. Baldengrumpy set it on a table at the front with a sniff of disgust.

"Now *don't* interrupt my lesson again, young man," he warned.

Stanley wanted to point out that he wasn't the one who interrupted in the first place—that actually he had done his best to cover things up so they could all carry on with the lesson like nothing happened. But something about the look on Mr. Baldengrumpy's face told him there was no point splitting hairs.

As soon as Mr. Baldengrumpy turned back to the chalkboard, Felicity looked around and stuck her tongue out at Stanley.

IT WAS A LITTLE WHILE LATER THAT STANLEY'S
school day *really* took a turn for the worse.

The trouble started halfway through first period,
when Mr. Baldengrumpy brought out a projector. The
class cheered. They were going to watch a movie!

Mr. Baldengrumpy explained he had a science film for them called *Our Neighbor, the Moon*.

The class groaned. Did he have to ruin *everything* by making it so "educational"?

But Mr. Baldengrumpy just started the film any-way and sat down at his desk to pretend to mark homework. Within minutes he had dozed off behind a stack of books and the whole class was educated half out of their minds.

"If I was any more educated, I'd be in a coma," grumbled Fiona. "Why do we have to watch this?"

"This is the lamest space movie ever," griped Kathleen. "When are they gonna blow something up with lasers?"

"Shhhh!!!" hissed Felicity, hunched over a notebook taking color-coded notes.

Stanley, meanwhile, was doing his best to pay attention to the movie because he didn't want to get in any more trouble with his teacher.

So nobody noticed when the small stuffy on the edge of the front desk, illuminated by an image of the full moon, twitched one floppy bunny ear and shivered like someone stirring from sleep. . . .

Slowly, one of its eyes blinked open, gazing straight ahead with a cold blank stare....

Stanley was finding it hard to concentrate on the film. Normally he loved space movies, but this one was seriously lacking in the freaky-aliens-with-death-rays department. It was just a lot of boring moon footage with a voice droning out such fascinating facts as how many paper cups you would have to stack one on top of the other to reach the moon.

Stanley wondered how they figured that out. He imagined a team of space scientists stacking paper cups day after day. They would've needed really tall ladders.

Suddenly, though, a shriek from the desk in front of him shattered his concentration.

"Mr. Baldengrumpy!" Felicity wailed. "Stanley's doll just *bit* me!"

MR. BALDENGRUMPY STOPPED THE MOVIE. SOME-
body flicked on the lights.

Zombiekins was sitting motionless on the edge
of the front desk. Just a harmless stuffy, albeit with a
somewhat macabre, half-dead appearance. But Felicity shrank from it in terror, holding her math book in
front of her like a shield.

"I-it bit me right here," she claimed, pointing to a spot on the back of her wrist.

There wasn't a mark, as far as Stanley could see, but naturally Mr. Baldengrumpy believed her anyway.

SPUTTER CLOSE UP

"I suppose this is your idea of a joke?" Mr. Baldengrumpy sputtered. Sputtered means he said it in an angry voice and emphasized his point by showering Stanley with spit droplets.

"I-I didn't—" Stanley stammered. "I-I never—"

But Mr. Baldengrumpy wasn't even listening. He just carried Zombiekins to his desk at the back of the room, muttering something about how he "should've gone to law school like Mother wanted." Then he told the class to take out their math books.

"Aw, what about the rest of the movie?" moaned Fiona.

"Now we'll never know how it turns out," groaned Kathleen.

But Mr. Baldengrumpy was always cranky when he didn't get his nap. He assigned the class three pages of word problems and the children moaned in agony—which seemed to cheer him up a bit.

From across the room, Miranda gave Stanley a questioning look. What was going on?

Stanley shrugged, then pointed at Felicity and made the crazy sign with his finger. Obviously she

was making the whole thing up. There was no way Zombiekins could've actually bitten her.

Was there?

Stanley remembered the Widow's mysterious warnings ("*Zat is no ordinary toy. . . .*") and turned to look back at his teacher's desk. . . .

But Zombiekins had disappeared!

Quickly, Stanley pushed his pencil off the edge of his desk and bent down to pick it up—just in time to see Zombiekins shuffling out of the classroom through the hall door. . . .

STANLEY STOOD UP AND SIDLED
over to the pencil sharpener by the
front door, counting on his fingers
in his best impersonation of a boy
embroiled in a math problem. He waited
until Mr. Baldengrumpy wasn't looking, then snatched a bathroom pass and
slipped out into the hall.

He didn't see Zombiekins, so
he ducked into the nearest cubby and crouched
behind some coats.

Once he was sure he wasn't being
watched, he darted from his cover—dove—
rolled—scrambled to his feet
in another cubby across the

hall—and pressed himself against the wall to catch his breath.

Then, from hiding place to hiding place, he zigged, zagged, crept, crawled, slipped, slunk, tumbled, stumbled, hopped (stubbed toe), and vaulted down the hall, moving like a cat. Like an extremely paranoid cat. He swooped, shimmied, slithered on his elbows, pounced, prowled, paused to wipe a mashed-banana stain from his shirtfront, hunched, hurdled, wriggled, wormed, tiptoed, leapfrogged, somersaulted, sprang, and—

*BONK!*ed his head on a lunch box straightening up.

Why was Stanley being so sneaky?

No reason. This was just how he always went to the bathroom

65

at school. You should've seen him fetch the atten-
dance register.

He was crawling on his hands and knees across
the floor, concealed under a yellow raincoat to avoid
attracting suspicion, when the door to the grade 6
class opened. Thinking quickly, Stanley jumped to
his feet and disguised himself as part of a display project on Egypt.

He held his breath as the sixth graders filed past
on their way to the library.

Last in line was Knuckles. He slouched by without giving Stanley a second glance. But halfway down the hall he stopped and sniffed the air like a jungle cat scenting its prey.

Stanley thought for sure he'd been discovered. But Knuckles just grunted, shook his head, and lumbered ahead to catch up with his class.

When the sixth graders had gone, Stanley searched their empty classroom ... the rest of the hall ... the boys' bathroom. . . .

But there was no trace of Zombiekins anywhere.

Stanley was baffled. It was as if Zombiekins had just vanished. The rest of the classroom doors were closed, and he'd checked everywhere else it could possibly...

Unless...

No...

Stanley tried to push the thought from his mind. It was too, too awful.

Not that...Anything but that...

A MOMENT LATER, STANLEY FOUND HIMSELF
sneaking into the girl's bathroom. He kept his eyes
trained on the floor and shaded
them with one hand so
he wouldn't accidentally
glimpse anything too
psychologically damag-
ing. He knew he must be
surrounded by millions of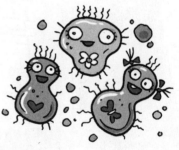
tiny girl germs and made a note to decontaminate
himself at recess by rolling in some dirt.

But it wasn't long before Stanley's curiosity
started to get the better of him and he peeked around
between a couple fingers. . . .

Stanley had always expected it would be like his Mom's bathroom at home—little flower-shaped soaps you weren't supposed to use, frilly towels that were only for show, that thick perfumey smell that always made him sneeze. . . .

But actually it was a lot like the boys' bathroom. He started to relax a little.

And that's when the door to the hall swung open behind him!

Stanley spun around in a flood of embarrassment—which quickly turned to terror—

For there, standing in the doorway, was Knuckles!

"I thought I smelt you sneaking around in here," Knuckles grunted. "Weirdo."

"I-I was just looking for something. . . ." Stanley stammered.

Knuckles took two menacing steps toward Stanley and the door closed behind him. The noise it made in the echoey bathroom was like the stone door to a tomb slamming shut.

"You shouldn't be in here, Nudelman," he sneered, coming closer. "What if something bad was to happen to you? Ha, ha. . . ."

Stanley backed away in terror, cursing himself for letting Knuckles catch him off guard twice in the same day. But before Stanley could slip past Knuckles by creating a diversion, flee the building, change his name and move to Australia, Knuckles grabbed hold of him again.

And the next thing Stanley knew, his head was wedged under Knuckles' armpit and he was staring down into a gleaming white toilet bowl.

"You know," Knuckles said in a reflective tone, "I almost feel bad about this. . . ."

"R-r-really?" Stanley squeaked, a faint hope stirring inside him.

"Naw," Knuckles sneered, pushing Stanley forward.

What happened next was all a blur. One moment Stanley was staring helplessly down at his own terrified reflection getting larger and larger...

Then a weird noise rang in his ears:

Stump!—scri-i-i-i-itch...

Knuckles stood up, yanking Stanley back. They both froze, listening. The noise echoed around the room like a rubber ball bouncing off all the walls. When it finally died out, they heard it again. Only this time it was closer:

Stump!—scri-i-i-i-itch...

Whatever was making the strange noise was in the next stall over—and sounded like it was dragging itself toward them!

Then they saw it....

Stump!—scri-i-i-i-itch...

From under the partition between the stalls it came... Staggering slowly toward them ... Moving stiffly, with a pronounced limp....

It was...

Zombiekins!!!

Obviously.

Like, *duh*.

Still, it was a shock. Even Stanley found the sight of it a little unsettling: The cold, dead eyes . . . the fierce, sharp fangs. . . the one floppy bunny ear. . . .

"Hey, isn't that your *doll?*" Knuckles snorted in a mocking tone—but Stanley heard a nervous tremor in his voice too. "Why's it following us like that?"

Knuckles backed out of the stall, dragging Stanley with him. Zombiekins just turned sharply and continued lurching in their direction.

"I-I don't know," Stanley replied. "I never even realized it was battery-powered."

Soon they were backed up against a wall and Knuckles was holding Stanley in front of him like a shield. Still Zombiekins kept coming.

"Make it stop, Nudelman," Knuckles whimpered. "Seriously, or else I'll—hunh?!"

Zombiekins latched onto Knuckles' pant leg.

"Get it off me!" Knuckles screamed, sliding down the wall. "Get it—AAAHHHHHHH!!!"

As Knuckles crumpled to the floor, his grip loosened and Stanley was able to break free and step away. . . .

Knuckles' eyes bulged and his mouth gaped open, but the only sound that came out was a sort of strangled gurgling—as if he was too choked with terror to scream.

For a moment, Stanley stood frozen in shock. Then, coming to his senses, he turned and bolted for the door. Behind him, the bathroom echoed with piteous smacking, smooching, puckering noises....

Stanley broke out into the hall just as Knuckles suddenly found his voice:

STANLEY BURST INTO HIS CLASSROOM. HIS HEART was pounding. His breath came in great heaving gulps. His head was spinning with everything he'd just seen....

But his classmates were just working quietly at their desks. Nobody even noticed him come in.

"... Agahgahgrrraaghagahgrraaghllhh ..."
Knuckles' wail echoed through the hall behind him.

Stanley started to slam the door, then caught himself and shut it carefully, with a tiny click.

Mr. Baldengrumpy looked up from his desk at the back.

Knuckles' screams went on and on, muffled only slightly by the door.

"...agahgahgahgahgahgahg ..."

Mr. Baldengrumpy gave Stanley a narrow look.

"You weren't *running in the halls* just now, were you?" he asked accusingly.

"N-no, sir," Stanley panted.

"I hope not," Mr. Baldengrumpy replied, in a voice like he didn't for one minute believe it. "Because you know we don't run in the halls."

Stanley waited for him to say more, but Mr. Baldengrumpy just went back to writing F's on the students' art assignments.

So Stanley went and sat down at his desk.

"*Mrmmrngmrmarnnnnn...*" Felicity mumbled to herself in front of him. Stanley couldn't make out what she was saying and didn't bother to ask. He had way too much running through his mind.

Somebody should check to make sure Knuckles was all right, Stanley thought. For a moment he considered telling his teacher what had happened....

"*Mrmmrngmrmarnnnnn...*"

No, obviously he wasn't thinking clearly. Mr. Baldengrumpy would never believe him. And even if he did, he'd only find some way to blame it all on Stanley.

"*Mrmmrngmrmarnnnnn...*"

Anyway, Zombiekins was just a toy. Surely it wouldn't actually *hurt* Knuckles.

But there was definitely *something* weird going on here. Stanley decided to talk to Miranda about it at recess. She always knew what to do.

As soon as he had made up his mind, Stanley felt a lot calmer and he was able to focus on pretending to do his work again.

"*Mrmmrngmrmarnnnnn...*"

Except now Stanley noticed for the first time that Felicity had been moaning to herself ever since he sat down. Stanley jabbed her in the shoulder with his pencil stub.

"Hey," he whispered. "Keep it down."

Felicity started turning around to face him. But her movements were weirdly stiff and slow, and her shoulders didn't turn at all. Her head just swiveled around, inch by inch, with a noise like an old gate creaking....

She was so changed Stanley hardly recognized her: Her eyes were clouded over like gray marbles. Her skin was the color of clam chowder. Her hairstyle was askew.

"Are you all right?" Stanley asked in shock.

He could tell there was something seriously wrong with her. Felicity would *never* let her hair get like that.

But she didn't answer him. She just moaned again and slowly, as if it took enormous effort, reached one hand up—

—and grabbed Stanley by the throat!

"Hey—" Stanley gasped, choking out the words. "—are you—crazy?!"

But Felicity just stared right through him with blank, clouded-over eyes.

"All right class," Mr. Baldengrumpy announced in a bored tone from his desk at the back, "put away your books and get ready for recess."

Kids sprang out of their seats, leaped into the aisles, danced, pranced, romped and gamboled to get their things and line up. Felicity lifted Stanley up out of his chair by the neck and shook him.

Sophia frolicked out to the hall to get her coat. Lydia skipped into line at the door. Jack twirled into the hall on his tippy-toes. Big Tony bounded to the front of the class to get a skipping rope from the box of recess toys. Fiona and Kathleen pushed and shoved to grab the hardest bouncy ball to use for murderball. Felicity bashed Stanley's head against his desk like she was trying to crack open a coconut.

"Stanley Nudelman," Mr. Baldengrumpy barked impatiently from the back. "Stop fooling around and get ready for recess."

Stanley tried to call to him for help, but all that came out was "Gack!" and "Hlp!"

"And don't *mumble*," Mr. Baldengrumpy scolded. "You really must learn to speak up."

Stanley couldn't breathe. . . . He felt himself starting to black out. . . .

But then the bell rang. As soon as it did, Felicity dropped Stanley to the floor and started lurching obediently out to recess.

Stanley lay on the floor, gasping and rubbing his throat.

"Hurry up, Stanley," Mr. Baldengrumpy said gruffly. "You'll never amount to anything in this world until you learn to walk quietly in a straight line with everybody else."

"I'M TELLING YOU, SHE'S A ZOMBIE."

"Stanley," said Miranda, "you've always had a pretty wild imagination, but this time you've finally gone nuts. Zombies only exist in the movies."

"Oh, yeah?" Stanley said. "Look at her. That's all she's been doing all recess."

Normally Felicity liked to spend her recesses holding the duty teacher's hand and tattling on kids who were breaking nitpicky safety rules like no climbing fences, no running up the slide, and no using the teeter-totter as a human catapult.

"She's just being stuck up," Miranda said.

"Okay, so what about Knuckles?" Stanley asked. "You should've heard him screaming."

Stanley shuddered just remembering it.

"That only proves what I've been telling you all along—that he's really just a big chicken baby," Miranda said. "Look, Stanley, Zombiekins is just a toy. There's no way it could actually hurt kids."

"I know what I saw," Stanley insisted. "There, look at her now—"

Felicity was lurching out onto the soccer pitch.

"So? Maybe she wants to play soccer."

"And risk getting a speck of dirt on her pretty, pretty dress?" Stanley said. "You know how she feels about 'perspiring.'"

"Okay, so maybe she is acting a little weird," Miranda admitted. "But that still doesn't make her a zombie."

Someone booted the soccer ball and it drilled
Felicity in the side of the head. She didn't even flinch.

The kids stopped playing soccer and crowded
around Felicity to ask if she was all right. But she just
stood there, swaying slightly, without replying. Then
she stooped over, picked up the soccer ball, and held
it out in front of her as if she'd never seen anything
like it before.

"See?" Stanley said. Even Miranda was starting to look doubtful.

Once the kids around Felicity realized she was okay, they started bugging her to give the ball back so they could get on with their game.

But Felicity just opened her mouth wide . . . and shoved the ball in!

15

FINALLY MIRANDA BELIEVED STANLEY.

"You keep Felicity out of trouble," she told him on the way up to class. "And I'll go check the girls' bathroom for Zombiekins and Knuckles."

"What do you mean, 'Keep her out of trouble?'" Stanley said, looking over his shoulder in alarm. "She wants to *eat* me."

Felicity was five places behind Stanley in line. When he turned to look back, she snarled, gnashed her teeth, and stretched a clutching hand out toward him. But fortunately she

wouldn't leave her place in line to get him.

"Stanley," Miranda said, lowering her voice confidentially, "do you have any idea how much trouble you'll be in if Mr. Baldengrumpy finds out *your toy* turned her into a zombie? You've got to keep her from doing anything to draw attention to her, uh, *condition*."

And with that, Miranda ducked out of line and hurried up the stairs.

Just ahead of Stanley, Fiona was dangling a worm in Big Tony's face.

"Ewwww!" screamed Big Tony. "Get it away from me!"

Fiona giggled and, with Kathleen egging her on, flung the worm at Big Tony. It stuck to the front of his shirt. He let out a piercing shriek, then danced and squirmed and slapped at his clothes like someone on fire until the worm finally shook loose and dropped onto the stair.

Fiona and Kathleen doubled over laughing. The rest of the line just kept trudging up the stairs.

Except Felicity. When she came to the worm, she stopped and pounced on it.... She rose up, holding it out in front of her...then popped it into her mouth and swallowed!

The line stopped and the noisy stairwell fell silent. Everyone stared at Felicity. Big Tony put his hand over his mouth like he was going to be sick.

It was a tense moment. Stanley knew he had to do

something to cover up before his classmates started to get suspicious.

"Uh, three-second rule?" he shrugged.

The other kids looked at him as if he was mental. Except for Fiona and Kathleen, who just nodded their heads and stared at Felicity with surprised admiration.

"Cool," said Kathleen.

ONCE THEY REACHED THE TOP FLOOR, THE LINE broke up, and kids scattered off in all directions to their cubbies. Felicity came shuffling after Stanley, lurching slowly and stiffly like... well, like a zombie....

He barely had time to dig his homework out of his knapsack, check that his mom had signed it, change into his indoor shoes, tie them in double knots, zip up his bag, open it again to grab a pencil from his pencil case, close it again, and narrowly escape before Felicity reached him.

Stanley took his seat inside the classroom and Felicity came staggering straight toward him, barging between the desks instead of taking the aisles. That's when Stanley realized he had a BIG problem: No matter how slow-moving Felicity was, as long as he stayed put she'd eventually catch him. But he couldn't run away without getting in trouble for being out of his desk.

Felicity kept lumbering in his direction . . . gnashing her teeth . . . clawing the air. . . .

Soon she was just a few lurches away. . . .

Stanley weighed his options: Mauled by a zombie? Or yelled at by his teacher?

He shrunk down as small as he could make himself at his desk. He decided he was more afraid of Mr. Baldengrumpy.

The next moment, Felicity was hovering right over him and Stanley was leaning way, way back to avoid the clutching hands that stretched ... toward ... his ... neck. ...

"Okay, class," Mr. Baldengrumpy droned. "Take your seats."

Felicity stopped and stiffened; her grip was cold as stone around Stanley's throat.

She unclenched his neck, shuffled ahead, and thumped down in her chair. As soon as she was seated, she swiveled her head around to hiss and bare her teeth at Stanley.

"Who would like to hand out the books?" Mr. Baldengrumpy asked.

Felicity's head swiveled to the front again. Her arm shot into the air, stiff and grasping, like a hand reaching up out of a freshly dug grave.

"*Mrmmrrngmrrmarnnnnn…*" she moaned loudly.

"Thank you, Felicity," said Mr. Baldengrumpy, setting the books down on her desk.

ELSEWHERE IN THE SCHOOL, IT WAS CENTER TIME
downstairs in Ms. Mellow's kindergarten and the
classroom was bustling with non-gender-specific
role-playing activities. Little girls in red firefighter
hats were tearing around making siren noises, filling
buckets at the Water Station and splashing them on a
pretend fire at the Computer Station. Little boys were

at the Craft Table, eating crayons and glue. In the Playhouse, one boy was pretending to be the kind of daddy who liked to wear an apron and bake mud pies, while the girl he was playing with was pretending to be the kind of mommy who liked to throw dishes and yell at you to get a job.

And in the middle of the busy room, one child stood all by himself, picking his nose with intense concentration.

In the sandbox, a little girl with pigtails was trying to soothe a little boy who was crying. He was crying because she'd just whacked him over the head with her plastic spade.

"There, there," said the little girl with pigtails, patting the boy on the shoulder. And when that didn't work, she dumped a pail of sand on him.

Over in the Story Corner, two boys who both wanted to read the same book were having a tug-of-war.

"Now, boys," Ms. Mellow chimed in a soothing singsong. "Remember, we always *share*."

Ms. Mellow's voice was so calm and sweet, it worked on the children like a spell: As soon as they heard her, the two boys stopped fighting and put the book scraps down on the floor where they could both read them together, with all the words and pictures upside down. And the kid who was picking his nose stopped and offered some to a girl who was bashing toy trucks together nearby.

At the back of the room, a small boy with glasses was playing by himself in the Doll Corner. Little Georgie liked to play with dolls, and there was nothing wrong with that. He liked to talk to himself in different voices and pretend it was the dolls talking, and there was nothing wrong with that. He liked to make the dolls scream in terror and rip each other limb from limb in a murderous rampage with the gnawing and the clawing and the gnashing and the smashing. . . .

And there was nothing wrong that.

Little Georgie was piling all the dollhouse furniture into barricades when he noticed a strange new toy staggering toward him from out of the coatroom.

It was some sort of stuffy, like a cross between a teddy bear and a stuffed bunny. Except it had fangs like the pointy bit on an electric can opener, claws as sharp as fishhooks, and something unnerving about its eyes.

"Ooo," Little Georgie exclaimed. "Cute."

Little Georgie picked up the weird toy. But as he cradled it in his arms, it wriggled and stretched its mouth toward his neck. . . .

"Aaaaaah!!!" Little Georgie squealed. "Nooooooooooo!!!"

Suddenly the Doll Corner rang with loud, piteous smackings and smoochings.

"Oo—ahh—STOP—ughh!!!" Little Georgie choked. "THAT—oo—ahh—arr—TICKLES—urrff!!!!"

A few minutes later, the little girl with pigtails got bored of burying the little crying boy in sand and came to see what Georgie was doing in the dollhouse.

"That doesn't go there," she said, lifting a sofa from one of Georgie's barricades. "It goes *here*."

She started removing all the furniture from Georgie's piles and placing it in the dollhouse rooms.

"And this goes here. . . . And this goes here . . . ." she said in a bossy tone.

"*Hmmgrgh...*" whimpered Georgie. He was hunched over, biting the head off a doll in a tuxedo.

"*I* want that," the little girl in pigtails said. She grabbed at Georgie's doll.

"*Mgnhrgnhhh,*" Georgie moaned, hugging it to his chest.

"*Give* it," the girl said. "You already had a turn."

She yanked and yanked until finally Georgie snapped at her, sinking his teeth into her wrist!

"Ow! I'm telling!" she threatened. "Ms. Mellow says you have to share, it's the–oo, I feel straaaaaange...."

The little girl with pigtails put her hand to her head. Her face turned gray. A dull, clouded-over look came into her eyes.

"I think I'm going to *hmmnrhghghrghgh...*"

UPSTAIRS, MEANWHILE, FELICITY KEPT MAKING hungry noises in Stanley's direction, but luckily she wouldn't leave her desk unless Mr. Baldengrumpy gave her permission.

Still, Stanley was afraid his teacher would notice something was wrong with her. Every time Mr. Baldengrumpy asked for volunteers to collect work or do chores around the room, she whimpered like a begging dog. And she bellowed with enthusiasm whenever he cracked a corny joke.

So in other words she was pretty much her usual self.

Except that her "work" was nothing but scribbles and at one point while washing the blackboard she chugalugged a box of chalk. Fortunately nobody noticed except Fiona and Kathleen, who just nodded in appreciation.

"Sick," Fiona complimented.

"Nasty," Kathleen praised.

When Miranda came back from checking the girls' bathroom, she gave Stanley a shrug from the door to let him know her search had come up empty. But they didn't get a chance to talk until halfway through the period, when on a secret signal they met at the pencil sharpener.

"The bathroom was empty," Miranda whispered. "So I searched the rest of the floor again—but there was no trace of Zombiekins anywhere."

"What about Knuckles?" Stanley asked with concern. "Was he with his class?"

"I don't know," Miranda shrugged. "The door to the sixth graders' room was closed."

"Something terrible has happened to him," Stanley said. "I just know it."

"Calm down, Stanley," Miranda said. "We don't know for sure that anything happened to Knuckles. So for now, let's just worry about keeping Felicity out of trouble. . . .

". . . and finding Zombiekins before anyone else does. . . ."

19

MEANWHILE, DOWN IN THE SCHOOL'S BASEMENT, the hall was filled with the sound of cats drowning to the tune of "Old MacDonald."

Mrs. Bernstein, the music teacher, was conducting the third graders. She stood at the front of the Music Room waving a conductor's baton with her eyes closed like someone in a trance.

To one side of the room, the string section was choking the cellos, battering the bass viols and doing violence to the violins. Across from them, the horn section was blaring like a traffic jam of angry cab drivers.

"Beautiful, boys and girls," Mrs. Bernstein beamed. "Marvelous!"

Underneath all this racket throbbed the dull haunting drone of Bubba on the tuba, who didn't know the tune and was blundering along with a noise like a ship lost in fog.

The kids all seemed to be enjoying themselves, especially Delores, who was doing air guitar moves on the ukulele, strutting and jiving and windmilling her strumming hand without really playing anything.

"Lovely, Delores!" Mrs. Bernstein cooed.

Mrs. Bernstein raised her baton to signal the finale was coming, then brought it down with a sharp flick. The tune tumbled to a halt with everyone finishing at different times and on different parts. Mrs. Bernstein clapped her hands together in delight.

"Bravo, everyone!" she sang. "That was fabulous!

"Okay," Mrs. Bernstein trilled, "let's try it again with a Latin feel...."

"Aw, can't we play 'Three Blind Mice'?" whined Jason.

"Pardon me, Jason?" Mrs. Bernstein smiled, removing a plug from her left ear.

"Why do we always have to play 'Old MacDonald'?" Jason complained. "Why can't we ever play 'Three Blind Mice'?"

"Or 'Hot Cross Buns'?" said Alycha.

"I wanna play 'Smoke on the Water'...."

"How about 'Ride of the Valkyries'?"

"All right, children," Mrs. Bernstein smiled, replacing her earplug. "You may all play whatever you like." She tapped her baton on the music stand. "On three..."

All the kids played their hearts out. Except for a girl named Mackenzie in the back row of the horn section. She had stopped playing momentarily to watch how the boy beside her produced such a wonderful tone from his trumpet—as if he'd trapped some strange animal inside that was screaming to get out.

That's why she was the only one who noticed when a strange stuffy appeared from behind a pile of violin cases by the door. It was small and creepy-cute and it moved on its own like something alive—or at least like something not quite dead.

Mackenzie watched, mesmerized, as the weird stuffy dragged itself along the floor, weaving through tapping feet, chair legs and music stands. It seemed to be heading straight for her, and as it got closer, she heard a faint noise under the racket of her classmates' playing:

Stump!—scri-i-i-i-i-itch ... **Stump!—scri-i-i-i-i-itch** ... **Stump!—scri-i-i-i-i-itch** ...

Soon the creepy-cute bunny monster had crossed the room. When it was almost at Mackenzie's feet, she bent down to pick it up. ...

SHORTLY BEFORE LUNCH, STANLEY SLIPPED OUT OF
class to search the school again while Miranda stayed
behind to watch Felicity.

He didn't find Zombiekins, but he did run into
Knuckles' class down in the gym. He knew it was
them by the horrible noises spilling out into the hall,
like the sounds from some medieval torture cham-
ber: Howls of pain ... Shrieks of terror ... Loud whaps
of slapping flesh ...

They were playing dodgeball.

Personally, Stanley hated dodgeball. He didn't
approve of games that involved targeting children
with dangerous projectiles. At least, he didn't approve
of games that involved targeting *him* with dangerous
projectiles. But Stanley's gym teacher Mr. Straap said

dodgeball was "character building" and made his class play it at least once a week.

Stanley halted outside the gym, listening to the horrifying racket: Foul curses and bitter threats. Battle whoops and warlike grunts. Desperate pleas and demonic laughter.

Obviously the sixth graders were enjoying themselves.

Stanley snuck onto the gym stage through the side entrance and hid behind a stack of gymnastic mats. It was the sixth graders, all right. The gym was a seething battlefield. Stanley winced as he watched one boy take a ball in the face from point-blank range.

"Owww!" the boy wailed, pinching his nostrils to stem the dripping blood. "I tink my doze id boken!"

"Walk it off, Toppleover," said Mr. Straap. "You're holding up the game."

But Knuckles was nowhere to be seen.

Stanley knew then that something awful must have happened to him. Knuckles wouldn't have missed dodgeball for *anything*.

Stanley slipped out into the hall again and was on his way back to class when something caught his eye. Around the corner from the gym was the Science Closet, where they stored stuff for science classes. Normally the room was kept locked at all times because teachers didn't want children getting into things and learning about science without supervision. But now Stanley noticed the door was open a crack. . . .

He gave the door a tiny, cautious push. . . .

It swung open with an eerie *creeeeeeak*—they always do—and Stanley took a deep breath and stepped inside. . . .

The room was windowless and dark, and the junk scattered on the floor and crammed onto shelves cast weird shadows on all the walls. Stanley took a few steps in—then jumped back when he felt a cobweb brush against his face. . . .

Fortunately, it turned out to be just a butterfly net hanging from a shelf.

Unfortunately, when Stanley jumped back he got tangled in a *real* cobweb. He thought he felt something large and hairy crawling down the back of his shirt. . . .

Stanley stood in the middle of the room, too afraid to move. All this spooky description was creeping him out. Then he thought he heard something...

Da-dum...da-dum...da-dum...

A steady thumping, like the music before something really bad happens in a scary movie...Stanley froze, listening as hard as he could....

Da-dum...da-dum...da-dum...

He couldn't tell where it was coming from, but it was definitely getting louder—and faster!

Da-dum—da-dum—da-dum—

Stanley felt a surge of terror—and the ominous music accelerated!

Dadum-dadum-dadum-dadum—

He wanted to scream but he was struck dumb with terror. The noise just kept building and building.... He didn't know which way to turn or where to run.... It seemed to be coming from right under—

Oh. Right.

Stanley put his hand on his chest.

It was just his heart beating.

He relaxed a little and the thumping quickly subsided.

But still, he was so creeped out he decided to get

out of there. He turned to go—and that's when he saw it!

Stanley felt woozy and had to lean up against the wall.

Oh, poor Knuckles! No matter how rotten he was, he didn't deserve this!

Stanley was flooded with memories of all the things he would've missed out on if it weren't for Knuckles: The recesses spent buried upside down in snowbanks. The nights padlocked to the bicycle rack.

The time he slalomed face-first down three flights of stairs lashed to a skateboard with skipping ropes. (Kids *still* talked about that.)

And now, after all they had shared together, *his* toy had done this to Knuckles. Stanley felt like he was going to be sick....

But suddenly a jolt of terror brought him to his senses. He had to get out of there, and fast—before the same thing happened to him!

He turned to flee—but the door creaked open behind him with a blinding flash that froze him to the spot!

"THERE YOU ARE. I'VE BEEN LOOKING ALL OVER for you."

When Stanley's eyes blinked back into focus, Miranda was standing in the doorway with her hand on the light switch.

"Don't come in!" he warned her. "Run! Save yourself!"

"What are you talking about?" Miranda asked.

"Look. . ." Stanley said, pointing to the gaping cadaver in the corner. But he couldn't bear to look himself.

"Yeah, so?" Miranda said. "What's the big deal?"

"WHAT'S THE BIG DEAL?!?" Stanley gasped. "How can you SAY such a thing? I mean, I know you never liked him, but—"

"What are you talking about?" Miranda asked.

"*What am I talking about*?" Stanley shouted. He never expected Miranda could be so coldhearted. "Just *look* at him!"

That's when he happened to sneak a peek over his shoulder himself....

Oops.

It wasn't Knuckles after all. It was only Cross-Section Guy from Health Class.

Stanley felt pretty foolish.

"Er, yeahhhhhh, just look at him," he repeated, trying to cover up his mistake. "I mean, look what somebody did to his vitals."

Cross-Section Guy had a brain jammed into his stomach cavity, a clump of intestines spilling out of his skull, and a balled-up pair of old gym socks where his heart should've been.

"Whatever," Miranda said, like she wasn't going to waste her time arguing with a nutcase. "Hurry up. We better check on Felicity."

Miranda tossed him his backpack—typically she had thought to bring it along—and together they headed for the school cafeteria.

"What were you crawling around in the dark for anyway?" Miranda asked as they weaved through the lunchtime crowds.

"Um, no reason," Stanley mumbled.

THE LUNCHROOM WAS FULL BY THE TIME STANLEY and Miranda arrived, but they had no trouble finding Felicity. She was sitting in front of a huge mound of food and a crowd of classmates were gathered around, watching her stuff one sandwich from the pile after another into her mouth: bologna, egg salad, peanut butter and jam, liverwurst and grape jelly. . . .

Kathleen and Fiona kept bringing more food and Felicity kept wolfing it down. She leaned forward and gobbled a tray of cold french fries without using her hands, like a pig rooting in a trough. She crunched and swallowed a turkey leg, bones and all. She tipped back a carton of coffee creamer and emptied it in a few gulps. Then she ate the carton.

Stanley and Miranda sat at a corner table by themselves. But when Stanley went to take out his lunch, there was nothing in his bag except the Widow's taffy. He had been so busy disposing of the evidence of Fetch's crime spree that morning, he must have forgotten to pack a lunch.

"Great," Stanley muttered. "First I accidentally turn Felicity into a zombie, now *this*."

"Listen, I've been thinking this over," said Miranda. "I bet this is all part of some game. You know how some dolls cry, or pee, or call you Mommy? Well, this one turns you into a zombie. It's supposed to be just for fun. "

"You think so?" Stanley asked.

"I'm sure of it," Miranda insisted. "And if I'm right, then there has to be some antidote that will turn Felicity back to normal once the game is over."

"Great!" Stanley said. "But how do we find out what it is?"

"Didn't the Widow say Zombiekins came with instructions? There must be something about the anti-dote in there."

Stanley gulped a piece of unchewed taffy down the wrong way.

"Um . . . er . . . yeah . . . uhhhhhhh . . . " he explained.

"Don't tell me you threw away the instructions? Oh, Stanley . . . "

"How was I supposed to know it turned kids into insatiable monsters?"

Over at Felicity's table, Butch handed Kathleen something blue and hairy in a plastic bag.

"I found this at the back of my desk!" he announced. "I think it's from first term!"

Kathleen took the hairy blue sand-wich from the bag and held it up with two fingers. Felicity craned forward like a baby bird and snatched it out of Kathleen's hand, accidentally nipping her finger, then gulped it down without chewing. (The sandwich, not the finger.)

"In that case," Miranda said, "I guess we just better hope we find Zombiekins before this gets any worse...."

THE PLAYGROUND OF DEMENTEDYVILLE ELEMENTARY at a few minutes before noon was a quiet, peaceful place, where squirrels darted to and fro across the pavement and butterflies fluttered lazily in the midday sun.

That is, until the recess bell rang.

Then the squirrels took to the trees, the butterflies dipsy-doodled it out of there for all they were worth, and all along the neighboring street little old ladies puttering in rose gardens dropped their pruning shears and hurried indoors to safety.

Because the first peal of the recess bell touched off a rumbling inside the school that rose and swelled like a gathering flood....

... Until all at once a tidal wave of children burst into the yard, pouring from all the doors and spilling out of windows. Suddenly the air was loud with the joyful sounds of children laughing, children singing, children shouting rude names as they raced to be the first to claim the foursquare courts and swings and the topmost branches of the tree nobody was supposed to climb in.

Over at the tetherball court, a freckly-faced boy and a tall girl with braces arrived together and grabbed the ball at the same instant.

"I was first," said the freckly-faced boy, with a tug.

"No, I was first," said the tall girl, with a yank.

Behind them, a line was already forming; kids were pushing and shoving to get closer to the front.

But then a shadow falling across the tetherball court made everyone look up....

The kids in line stopped jostling and stared with frightened eyes.... The tall girl let the tetherball slip through her hands and stepped back, shaking.... The freckly-faced boy let go too and backed away, quaking....

It was a pack of sixth graders—they always traveled in packs—and just the sight of them was enough to send the younger kids scurrying for cover. The boys wore black T-shirts, dark hoodies and permanent sneers, and their hair was an open rebellion against society and interfering mothers. The girls had improbable hair colors and makeup plastered on so thick they looked like ghoulish figures from a wax museum. Next to the kindergarteners, they were the scariest kids in the school.

One by one, all the children in line disappeared—except for one girl from third grade, who shuffled ahead

128

as the line melted away until finally she stepped up and took hold of the tetherball.

"Hey, kid, are you blind or something?" said a sixth grader who looked like a gorilla. "We're playing with that."

"Yeah, twerp, are you deaf or something?" said another sixth grader who smelled like a baboon. "Beat it."

The girl turned slowly and stiffly to face them. It was Mackenzie. She growled from deep in her throat, like a dog: *"Grrrrrrrrrr..."*

Gorilla Face and his friend with the baboon-fresh scent halted, like they didn't want to get any closer. But a couple of their classmates piped up behind them:

"Go play on the swings, pip-squeak," said a girl with blood-red fingernails.

"Yeah, go build a sand castle for your dollies, shrimp," said another girl with vampire-bat-black lips.

They shoved the boys from their class forward into Mackenzie—

And like a cornered animal, she snarled and lunged back at them.

"Ow! She *bit* me!" yelped Gorilla Face. "Great, now I'll probably have to get shots!"

"ALL I'M SAYING IS, SOMETHING BAD MUST'VE
happened to Knuckles," Stanley said, lining up a
free throw under the basketball net. "You know he
wouldn't miss dodgeball for anything."

"Stanley, I'm telling you, this is all just some kind
of game," Miranda said. "Zombiekins is still just a toy.
Sure, it turns kids into zombies—but it wouldn't actually *hurt* them."

A burst of screaming from the direction of the
tetherball court made Stanley flinch. His shot never
reached the backboard.

"Oh, yeah?" Stanley said. "Look what it did to
Felicity...."

"I don't know," said Miranda. "In some ways it's
an improvement...."

"Yeah, but that's just from one little bite," Stanley said. "What if Knuckles didn't get away so easily? *What if . . .*" Stanley added, lowering his voice, "*. . . he didn't get away at all?*"

"Oh, stop letting your imagination get so carried away," Miranda scoffed.

Stanley aimed his next shot—but just as he was launching it, a bunch of kids ran in front of him, and the ball slipped from his hands in a weak arcing lob.

"Aaaaaaaaaahhhh!!!!" the kids screamed as they stampeded past.

Stanley turned to give a dirty look to who-ever was chasing them . . .

. . .While his ball bounced limply off the back-board, rolled around the rim, then fainted through the hoop in exhaustion.

"*Nice shot!*" Miranda exclaimed.

But Stanley wasn't even looking. He was staring across the yard.

"The sixth g-g-graders . . ." he stammered. "They're . . . they're . . . *they're all zombies!*"

"How can you tell?" Miranda asked.

Sixth graders slouched and shuffled all over the playground, stiff-limbed, with pale, vacant faces and cold, lifeless eyes.

Speaking only in grunts or snarls, they trod on flowerbeds and barged through four-square games as though oblivious of their surroundings, attacking any kids who didn't get out of their way fast enough....

"So?" Miranda said. "They're always like that."

The recess bell rang. Instantly, the sixth graders stopped biting and mauling each other, lurched stiffly to attention, and started shuffling obediently into line by the door.

"Wonderful, Grade 6," Mrs. Plumdotty praised. "You're setting such a good example for the younger children."

Up and down the line, the sixth graders moaned and bellowed happily like petted dogs.

"You're right!" Miranda exclaimed. "They *are* a bunch of zombies!"

AS THE SIXTH GRADERS TRUDGED UP THE STAIRS, a slow-moving line of growling, grumbling monsters, all the younger children scattered from their path in terror. Not because the other kids realized they were zombies—just because they always stayed out of the sixth graders' way.

"Oh, man," Stanley whimpered as he climbed the stairs with Miranda. "I am in soooo much trouble."

"Don't panic," Miranda said. "As long as it's just the grade 6s, maybe no one will notice."

But an even bigger surprise was waiting for them when they reached the third floor....

All of their classmates had been turned into zombies! They staggered mindlessly around the room, bumping into desks and knocking over chairs. Sarah was licking the homework off the chalkboard. Carlos had his hand stuck in the pencil sharpener. Big Tony was sitting on the floor, mooing plaintively while zombie Fiona and zombie Kathleen whacked h i m with yardsticks.

Stanley and Miranda halted in the doorway, frozen with fear—terrified, that is, that their teacher would notice something out of the ordinary.

But when Mr. Baldengrumpy told the zombies to sit at their seats, they sat at their seats. When he told them to take out their books, they took out their books. And when he said, "Write your name at the

top of the page," all the zombies tried to write "Your Name"—but between their zombie handwriting and zombie spelling, he never noticed.

In fact, for the rest of the period, as far as Mr. Baldengrumpy was concerned, the zombies were model students. They didn't speak without raising their hands. Or interrupt his lessons with pesky questions. Or finish their work so quickly he had to find something else for them to do.

Still, Stanley and Miranda thought they would be discovered for sure when Mr. Baldengrumpy called on Marcus to do his oral presentation on "Personal Hygiene in the Middle Ages."

Marcus stood at the front of the class, slumped and swaying like a barn door off its hinges. He was holding a poster the wrong way up and drooling down his shirtfront.

"*Ummm hrng grgl ummm glrrrdddll umm . . .*" he groaned.

"*Stop right there!*" Mr. Baldengrumpy barked.

Stanley felt a surge of panic. He was certain his teacher had noticed something wrong.

"Start again," Mr. Baldengrumpy ordered. "And do it without the 'um's this time."

Next to kids who walked up the wrong side of the stairwell, there was nothing Mr. Baldengrumpy hated more than mumbly public speakers.

Marcus just stared back blankly, wobbling and drooling.

"*Hrng grgl glrrdd ngghrrr . . .*" he moaned.

"Much better," said Mr. Baldengrumpy.

Halfway through the period, Miranda signaled Stanley to meet her at the back of the room.

"This is out of control," she said. "We've got to find Zombiekins and bring it back to the Widow after school. Maybe she can tell us what the antidote is."

"But we can't both leave class to go search," Stanley pointed out. "There's only one bathroom pass."

At that moment, their classmate Bryce came staggering down a nearby aisle carrying a pair of scissors, tripped over a kleenex and fell on his face. Slowly and clumsily, he dragged himself to his feet and looked around for the scissors—but he couldn't find them because they were stuck in his chest.

"Somehow I don't think that's the worst of our problems right now, Stanley," Miranda said.

26

MIRANDA FIGURED THEY COULD SEARCH THE school faster if they split up, so she sent Stanley to look in the basement while she combed the top floors again. But when he got down there, the scene that confronted him stopped him in his tracks. The entrance to the kindergarten room was covered in blood-red smears!

Terrified of what he'd find, Stanley had to force himself to look inside....

All over the classroom, little zombies in pigtails and short-pants were scratching, strangling, bashing, biting, mugging and mauling each other. There were kinderzombies in the sandbox, burying one another in sand ... kinderzombies in the Story Corner, munching on their favorite books

... a crowd of kinderzombies clawing and drooling around a glass terrarium full of nervous caterpillars for the class butterfly project....

"Alice," Miss Mellow said in her usual calm honey tones, "we don't put Simon's head in our mouth."

In the middle of all this chaos, one little zombie stood patiently picking his nose—until a little girl zombie saw and lurched hungrily in his direction.

"*Mrhrnghrmdrn* ..." the little girl zombie groaned, choking him.

"*MRGHNHRRGLLRR!*" the little boy zombie roared, choking her back.

"Use your inside voices," Miss Mellow gently reminded them.

Stanley backed out of the classroom in horror. Behind him, the hall was filled with a shrill, tuneless racket coming from down by the Music Room. It sounded like mice squealing, crows shrieking, geese quarreling, cows bellowing, donkeys braying, cats hissing, snakes yodeling, and a dog with its tail stuck in a door.

"Wonderful, children!" Stanley heard Mrs. Bernstein shouting from inside. "Louder!"

Stanley knew before he looked that it would be just like the kindergarten class. Sure enough, the room was full of zombies: zombies munching on ukuleles, zombies banging violins against their music stands like hammers, zombies blowing into the wrong ends of their trumpets—and none of them following the tune at all, except for one pair in the corner who were bashing each other over the head with cellos in time with Mrs. Bernstein's baton....

It was the same upstairs in the gym where the third graders were playing floor hockey. They swarmed around the ball, battering one another with  their sticks, while Mr. Straap stood on the sidelines shouting encouragements.

"Good hustle, Speckley," he called as a tall girl hacked her way through a pack of classmates.

Another boy stumbled after the ball, dragging a weirdly bent and twisted leg behind him.

"That's it, Puffler," Mr. Straap cheered. "Don't give up on the play!"

But then one of the zombies inadvertently scored a goal and play was stopped while the goalie fished the ball out of the back of the net and ate a chunk of it.

BUT STANLEY AND MIRANDA DIDN'T FIND ANY SIGN of Zombiekins, and by the time they met up again at last recess, the playground was swarming with zombies. Some were just staggering around, aimless and vaguely menacing, like teenagers. Others were playing normal recess games—except their reflexes were so slow they got tangled up in skipping ropes, and games of catch turned into games of fetch, and every serve in foursquare bounced off somebody's chest and rolled across the yard out into traffic.

Stanley and Miranda were tossing a ball around by themselves at the back of the yard when two zombies stumbled through the flower garden beside them, choking and biting each other.

"Mind you don't trample the tulips, boys," tutted Mrs. Plumdotty.

"We have to tell her," Stanley said. "This is out of control."

"Tell her what? That you accidentally turned all the kids in school into zombies?" Miranda replied. "You'd be in detention till you're eighty."

Stanley noticed she didn't say "we."

"Let's just worry about finding Zombiekins for now," Miranda went on. "Then after school, we'll go ask the Widow about the antidote."

She tossed the ball lightly to Stanley, but it bounced through his legs and rolled away under the dumpster by the back fence.

"Don't worry," Stanley said reassuringly a moment later, lying on his stomach. "I see it."

It was dark and filthy as a cave under the dumpster but Stanley thought he could just make out a shadowy bump way at the back that might be a ball. He started to crawl under to get it. His head bumped against the bottom of the dumpster with a loud *thunk*!

Ouch! That smarted. Stanley shimmied forward, more carefully this time. But to his surprise the noise rang out again, like some strange, delayed echo: *thunk*!

And then again: *thunk*!

"Weird," Stanley mumbled, crawling further under.

Above him, there was a loud **skkkkrrrrrrrrkkkkk** like claws scratching on metal . . . then a *creeeeeakkk* like the lid of a dumpster opening. . . .

"Uhhh, Stanley . . ." said Miranda.

"Hold on," Stanley replied, stretching as far as he could. "I've—almost— "

"Stanley, you really ought to—"

But Stanley didn't catch the rest of her remark because it was drowned out by a low, vowelless growl: "*Mngrbrgngnlll...*"

"Got it!" Stanley announced triumphantly, backing out from under the dumpster and rising to his feet. He dusted off his shirtfront and proudly held out the dirt-covered ball.

But Miranda didn't even give it a glance. She was staring right past Stanley, her eyes wide with terror and fixed on something just over his shoulder....

Behind him, there was another growl: "*Mngrbrgngnlll...*"

This time Stanley started to turn around....

Rising slowly from the dumpster behind him was Knuckles. Pale as a corpse, with cold dead eyes and wild matted hair, drooling garbage juice down his chin, he looked even more like a monster than usual.

When Knuckles recognized Stanley, his zombie eyes flashed with rage—or maybe it was hunger. He spat out a mouthful of garbage and growled again, more distinctly: "*Mnaarrhaarbwragnagnylll....*" Then, slowly and awkwardly, Knuckles started climbing out of the dumpster.

Too scared to run, Stanley could only watch in horror as Knuckles hoisted himself over the side of the dumpster with stiff, clumsy movements—then lost his balance—teetered on the edge—and fell headfirst on top of Stanley!

28

"GET HIM OFF ME!" STANLEY BEGGED MIRANDA. "HE'S trying to kill me!"

Actually, Knuckles was sprawled motionless on his back on top of Stanley as though the fall had stunned him. But when Stanley started to squirm out from under him, Knuckles grabbed Stanley's leg.

"Don't let him intimidate you, Stanley," Miranda said. "This is your chance to stand up to him!"

But Stanley was in no position to stand up to anyone at that particular moment because Knuckles was dangling him off the ground by an ankle.

"Go on, Stanley, show him he can't push you around," Miranda urged as Knuckles pushed Stanley around, then pummeled him about, then ping-ponged him to and fro.

"Helllllllllp!" Stanley pleaded as Knuckles twirled him around and around. "Doooo somethinggggg!"

Miranda just shook her head.

"Okay," she said in a disappointed voice. "Keep him busy till I get back."

So Stanley kept Knuckles busy. First he seized hold of Knuckles' hand with his neck. Then he pounded Knuckles in the fist with his face. Then he bashed Knuckles in the knee with the side of his head.

Stanley was just lying down on the pavement to strike Knuckles sharply and repeatedly in the foot with his stomach when Miranda reappeared with a wooden baseball bat.

"What are you wait-ait-aiting for-or-or?" Stanley pleaded as Knuckles shook him upside down like someone trying to squeeze the last drop out of a ketchup bottle. "Hit him-im-im!"

"No, Stanley," Miranda said. "You have to be the one to do it. He'll never leave you alone until you show him you can stick up for yourself."

Knuckles flipped Stanley high in the air like a coin and Stanley slammed down on the pavement on his back. Taffy spilled from his backpack like a splatter of guts.

"You'll thank me for this later," Miranda insisted. "That is, unless...."

She trailed off without finishing, and with a little shrug, threw the bat to Stanley.

Before Knuckles could pick him up for another toss, Stanley sprang to his feet and backed away with it cocked over his shoulder.

"Stay back," Stanley warned. "I mean it."

Knuckles just kept staggering toward him, snarling and drooling and snapping his jaws in hungry chomping motions.

"Aim for the head," said Miranda. "It's the only way to stop a zombie."

Stanley's fingers tightened around the bat handle....

"Do it, Stanley," Miranda urged. "He's not Knuckles anymore...."

But Stanley just let the bat fall to his side. He couldn't do it.

And the next moment, Knuckles grabbed Stanley around the neck and started pulling him closer with his mouth stretched wide....

"Don't let him bite you!" Miranda shouted. "You'll be turned into a zombie!"

Stanley fought and squirmed, but Knuckles' grip was like iron . . . His teeth were inches from Stanley's neck. . . .

With his last drop of strength, Stanley swung the bat—

And with a loud *crack!*, it splintered against the side of Knuckles' head!

"Now, boys," Mrs. Plumdotty tutted. "Use words, not sticks."

Knuckles wobbled backward, holding his temples like someone with a splitting headache. He staggered to a halt in front of the swings. He growled at Stanley with eyes full of hate, bared his teeth, and lurched forward. . . .

Into the path of a zombie swooping down on the swings!

Knuckles was knocked backwards—toward the roundabout, which a couple other zombies were steadily and robotically spinning.

Knuckles' belt loop caught on the roundabout, and like someone sucked into a tornado, he spun around, and around, and around....

"Ouch!" Stanley winced. "*Turbo wedgie.*"

Stanley started sweeping the Widow's taffy back into his knapsack

"Did you see that?" Stanley bragged to Miranda. "That'll teach *him* to pick on Stanley Nudelman!"

"Uh-oh . . ." Miranda said beside him.

"'Uh-oh' what?" asked Stanley, looking up.

"Uh-oh *that*—"

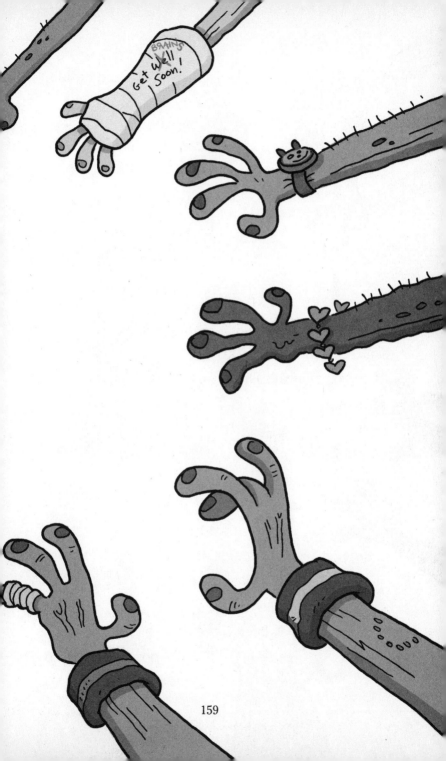

159

29

THEY WERE SURROUNDED
by an army of zombies. A
sea of zombies. Or a bunch
of them, anyway. All staring
at Stanley with blank, hungry
looks.

"*Hrnrgrghnrr*," remarked
one of the zombies.

"*Yarrghhhh*," commented another.

Then the whole crowd started *hrrgnghrr*ing and
*yaargh*ing—and suddenly they all surged forward,
snapping their jaws like hungry nestlings fighting over
a worm.

Stanley was cornered.

"The slide!" Miranda called to him
from the other side of the mob.

Zombies came grunting and groping, groaning and moaning, snapping and snarling toward Stanley on every side, closing in around him with their awful zombie eyes and their even awfuler zombie breath. . . .

Stanley started to back away and bumped up against the play structure—trapped!

He was zombie food. A Stanley sandwich. A lunch buffet for the walking dead. A—

Wait a minute. . . . What was Miranda doing on the *other* side of the mob?

"Use the slide," she repeated calmly. "Just climb up and escape down the slide."

In a flash, Stanley understood. Well, maybe it took a couple of flashes. Actually, maybe it was more like when you're trying and trying to take a photograph and finally somebody points out that you forgot to turn the flash *on*. But eventually Stanley figured it out; that's the important thing.

He spun around and started scrambling up the crisscrossing

ropes behind him. Zombies clutched and clawed at his legs, stretching their mouths to chomp into them like drumsticks. One got hold of his shoelace and started pulling Stanley back down with the strength of ten fourth graders. The mob below let out a hungry moan as Stanley slipped—back—toward them—

Luckily, his shoelace came untied and slid through the zombie's grasp. (Good thing he was never very good at tying double knots.) And

with the last of his strength, Stanley pulled himself to safety.

Stanley shimmied along a wooden beam toward the slide. A few of the zombies tried to follow him up the rope ladder but got tangled like fish in a net. The rest were so slow-moving and slow-thinking

that by the time they caught on what Stanley was doing, he had swooped down the slide to join Miranda.

But the two of them weren't out of trouble yet. They were still trapped in a playground full of zombies, cut off from the only gate leading out of the yard. And it wasn't long before the crowd under the play structure realized they'd been duped and came stumbling and staggering after them, moaning angrily.

Stanley and Miranda made a dash for the back door with the angry zombie mob right on their tail. Stanley barely had time to stop and tie his shoelace....

They reached the back door just as the recess bell rang....

"It's locked!" Miranda cried.

STANLEY YANKED AND yanked on the handle, but it was no use. He pounded on the door, but there was nobody inside to hear....

"I sent Russell in to open it," Mrs. Plumdotty said cheerfully, appearing beside them. "I wonder what's keeping him. I do hope he isn't dawdling."

By now every zombie in the whole playground was schlepping and schlumphing toward them—some chasing Stanley and Miranda, the rest just obediently staggering into line by the door.

"Mrs. Plumdotty, we have to get out of here!" Miranda blurted out. "These kids are all zombies!"

Stanley's heart sank. He knew they must be in bad trouble if Miranda was asking for help from a teacher.

"Now, Miranda," Mrs. Plumdotty replied, "you know it's not nice to call the other children names."

"No, you don't understand," Stanley hurried to explain. "She means they're flesh-eating monsters who want to guzzle our livers and gobble our limbs!"

"Stanley, dear, don't be such a tattletale," chided Mrs. Plumdotty.

Stanley and Miranda stood with their backs against the school wall, completely surrounded by moaning, groaning, grasping, grumbling zombies....

Suddenly the door beside them swung open and a little zombie stumbled out.

"*Hhrngghrghrgllng...*" the zombie groaned mindlessly.

"Thank you, Russell, dear," Mrs. Plumdotty said.

And before the door could swing closed again, Stanley and Miranda ducked under a swarm of grasping zombie arms and dashed inside.

"Wait, dears!" Mrs. Plumdotty called after them. "I haven't sent your line in yet."

But Stanley and Miranda bolted up the stairs, not thinking where they were headed, just trying to put as much distance as possible between themselves and the horde of zombies already filing into the stairwell behind them....

They reached the second floor landing, wheeled around without stopping, dashed up to the—

"A-*ha*!"

Standing at the top of the stairwell with a smug grin on his face was Mr. Baldengrumpy.

"Up to your usual tricks, Isee,"hescolded,shakinghishead. "Well, you can just march right back down there and come up again on the other side!"

Behind them, zombies were streaming up the stairs in an endless line, like ants. As soon as they caught sight of Stanley and Miranda, they all growled and gnashed their teeth.

"But, but—we'll be torn to pieces!" Stanley pleaded. "We'll be eaten alive—or worse, turned into mindless automatons devoid of all independent thought and free will!"

"Maybe then you'll learn to follow the rules," Mr. Baldengrumpy said unbudgingly.

So Stanley and Miranda had no choice but to trudge back down into the mass of mawing, clawing zombies. The zombies growled and snarled. They gnashed their teeth. They groped and grasped with clawlike fingers. But fortunately for Stanley and Miranda they wouldn't leave their side of the stairs to get them.

At the bottom of the stairwell, though, a logjam of zombies was blocking the door to the playground. Stanley and Miranda saw they would never get through.

"Quick—this way!" Miranda said, pulling Stanley back up the stairs. "I have an idea...."

The second-floor hallway, where the primary classrooms were, was crawling with zombie first graders and zombie second graders. Pale as corpses, with dead soulless eyes and mouths full of dark yawning gaps where they'd lost their baby teeth, they were a terrifying sight—or might have been, except that the tallest of them barely came up to Stanley's shoulder.

Stanley and Miranda burst into the hall. For a moment, the first and second graders just stopped and stared. Then, with a great howl, they all set upon Stanley and Miranda like a pack of wild dogs—small ones, jumping up on them and nipping at their elbows.

Stanley and Miranda fought their way through the mob, made a dash toward the heavy fire doors at the end of the hall, and escaped while all the grade 1s and 2s stopped to change into their indoor shoes like good little zombies.

Beyond the doors, the hall branched off to the right, and Stanley followed Miranda past the Library, the Computer Lab....

"Where are we going?" he asked. "This hallway is a dead end."

"Not exactly," Miranda said, stopping in front of the door at the end of the hall. "Come on, they'll never think to look for us in here."

"Oh, no . . ." Stanley hesitated. "Not there . . . We can't. . . ."

They heard the fire doors open behind them and a stampede of shuffling footsteps approaching around the corner. Miranda shoved Stanley through the door and slammed it shut behind them....

"QUICK!" MIRANDA SAID. "HELP ME MOVE THIS SOFA."

Together they dragged a ratty old sofa across the room and pushed it up against the door. Then they piled everything they could find on top of it: stacks of vacation catalogs, huge dusty piles of unmarked homework they uncovered when they moved the sofa, all the furniture in the room that wasn't too heavy to move....

"Ew," said Stanley, "there's chewing gum stuck under all these chairs."

On the other side of the door, the noise kept building until it sounded like there was a stampede of angry cattle mooing and mulling out in the hall.

Stanley and Miranda took cover behind a table at the back of the room as the clamor reached its peak. The zombies were right outside the door!

"*Mmmhhrrgh!*" roared one of them.

"*Nnyyyarrghrggl!*" raged another.

There was a pause.

"*Mrrghhr?*" groaned another zombie, more puzzled than angry.

Stanley held his breath, hoping they would give up looking and go away. But the next moment, the sound of the door handle jiggling made his blood freeze—they were trying to get in!

One of them started pounding on the door...

Then another... and another...

Until soon the door shook with a thunder of thumping and battering that rattled all the junk heaped against it and stirred up a dust cloud from the pile of unmarked homework...

But their barricade held.

After a few tense moments, the pounding stopped. Gradually the angry voices dimmed. There was a shuffling of feet outside in the hall, then that too fell silent.

"I think they've gone back to class," Miranda whispered.

"Phew!" Stanley sighed. "Now let's get out of here and go ask the Widow for help."

"No, hold on," Miranda said. "I think we should wait here till school is over and they've all gone home."

Stanley started to object, but Miranda explained:

"It's the perfect hideout," she went on. "In all the zombie movies I've ever seen, the heroes always hole up somewhere just like this. Somewhere with only one way in, where you'd never expect the zombies to find them...."

"But what if they *do* find us?" Stanley asked. "Doesn't that mean there's only one way *out*, too?"

"Oh, they always find you," Miranda said, matter-of-factly. "But trust me, this is just the way it's done."

Stanley couldn't argue with her. He never watched

scary movies because they made him see monsters in the shadows cast by his nightlight for weeks after.

So they tried to relax and look for ways to pass the time until school was over. Miranda went around checking the windows for an escape route, but they'd all been sealed shut to prevent teachers from climbing out onto the ledge on rainy days when the chil- dren were kept indoors for recess.

As for Stanley, now that he wasn't being chased by flesh-eating zombies, he realized he was pretty hungry himself. He never did get a proper lunch, after all. But even though the Teach- er's Lounge was full of old pizza boxes and empty glasses with little umbrellas in them, he couldn't find a crumb of anything to eat. Finally he got so desper- ate he decided to eat some of the Widow's taffy from his knapsack.

"Hey," Stanley said, peeling the wrapper off a piece of taffy with a loud *rrrrrrrip*, "how come we never thought to look for Zombiekins in here?"

As soon as the words left Stanley's mouth, an awful thought struck him. He tried to push it out of his mind—but he could tell by the way Miranda was staring back at him that the same idea had just occurred to her....

And then, from somewhere nearby in the room, with timing so pat it was downright eerie, they heard it:

Stump!—scri-i-i-i-i-itch ...

From out of a broom closet by the door, Zombiekins appeared....

Stump!—scri-i-i-i-i-itch ...

Slowly but steadily, Zombiekins advanced across the room toward them, one leg dragging like a dead limb....

Stump!—scri-i-i-i-i-itch . . .

Slowly but steadily, it came bearing down on Stanley and Miranda like some monster out of a horror movie. . . .

. . . Like some really short monster . . . Which also happened to be really slow . . .

But it wasn't long (well, not *that* long, anyway) before Zombiekins had crossed the room and was almost upon them.

Fortunately Stanley and Miranda managed to escape in the nick of time by taking a couple steps backward.

"W-what should we do?" Stanley asked Miranda.

"Catch it in your knapsack," Miranda said, inching back another step.

That had been their plan all along—but it didn't seem so easy now that they found themselves trapped in a room with a killer teddy.

Zombiekins just kept dragging itself steadily after them, and Stanley and Miranda kept edging away, and edging away, until finally on their third lap around the room Miranda made a suggestion.

"On second thought," she said, "maybe we *should* sneak out of school while the zombies are stuck in class...."

They made a dash across the room and started digging through the barricade, item by item.

Zombiekins turned and followed them, slowly and menacingly....

Stump!—scri-i-i-i-i-itch ...

"It's following us slowly and menacingly!" Stanley said.

They lifted chairs off the pile as fast as they could. Soon Zombiekins was just a few steps away.

Stump!—scri-i-i-i-i-itch ...

"It's just a few steps away!" Stanley shrieked.

"Don't panic!" Miranda said in a panicky voice, as she pushed the sofa aside and swung the door open—

"*Now* panic?" asked Stanley.

"Okay," Miranda muttered in shock. "I guess now you may as well go ahead and panic...."

FOR ONE TENSE MOMENT, STANLEY AND MIRANDA stared out at the mob staring in at them. Then, slowly, a flicker of understanding spread through the crowd— and with a sudden roar, all the zombies surged forward at once!

Miranda tried to slam the door, but it caught with a loud crunch of bone—a zombie at the front had jammed its arm in the crack!

"Quick," Miranda gasped, leaning into the door with all her might, "push the sofa back!"

Stanley did, then together they quickly piled the stacks of vacation catalogues and unmarked homework back on top. But already more grasping arms were writhing over the threshold, and Stanley and Miranda could see it was only a matter of time before their barricade gave way....

Then their barricade gave way.

There was a mighty push from the other side and the door flung open, toppling the sofa and sending holiday catalogues and unmarked math tests fluttering all over the room.

Stanley and Miranda backed away in helpless terror. There was nothing between them and the mob of bloodthirsty zombies now. . . .

Except that all the zombies tried to push through the doorway at once and got stuck.

It wasn't long, though, before they started squeezing one by one into the room. Soon they were closing in around Stanley and Miranda on all sides. Their eyes were blank and clouded over, their skin was gray and clammy—and, collectively, they really could've used a breath mint.

Backed against the far wall, Stanley and Miranda looked around desperately for some weapon to fend the zombies off with. But there was nothing. Then Miranda's glance fell on the piece of unwrapped taffy Stanley was still holding and a strange look came into her eye.

"Hey, what if . . ." she muttered to herself, as if an idea had just occurred to her. "Quick, Stanley, give me your knapsack!"

Stanley passed it to her, thinking she was going to swing it at the zombies. Instead, she plunged her hand inside and brought out a handful of the Widow's taffy.

"Try throwing this at them," she said, tossing the knapsack back. "I have a hunch it might slow them down...."

She wound up and hit the first zombie square between the eyes. The zombie didn't even flinch, and the candy bounced harmlessly to the floor.

Stanley thought Miranda was crazy, but she wouldn't give up. She just kept pelting the oncoming hordes with taffy, hitting one zombie after another.

Meanwhile, the first zombie stopped and stared

at the taffy lying at its feet. Slowly, he bent forward, picked it up, and tore the wrapper off with clumsy fingers. He stood for a moment gawking at the hard brown lump—then popped it into his mouth.

There was a crack and crunch of breaking teeth as the zombie chewed....

And chewww-wwwed...

And chewww-wwww-wwww-www-wwwwed...

Miranda was right—the Widow's taffy *was* slowing him down!

All around the room, other zombies had stopped to pounce on the candy. Some started fighting over it, bashing and choking each other for a piece.

Whatever Miranda's plan was, Stanley thought, it looked like it was working—at least for the moment.

He dug some more taffy out of his knapsack and started flinging the stuff like mad along with her.

But then, from out of the crowd of wrangling-strangling-biting-fighting-smashing-bashing zombies came Zombiekins itself, staggering toward them....

Stanley and Miranda shrank back in terror.

"Oh, no!" Miranda said. "Just when it looked like we might make it after all...."

The note of hopelessness in her voice gave Stanley a chill. Miranda was the one who always bailed them out of jams—if she was giving up, they were done for.

At least, that was the first thought to pass through Stanley's mind. But the next moment, it was as if a strange change came over him. Maybe it was that everything he had been through that day had stirred something unsuspected deep inside him. Or maybe it was just that even a boy like Stanley can be pushed only so far.

But whatever it was, Stanley puffed his chest out in a superhero pose and stepped out from behind Miranda.

"Cover me," he said, his voice straining a little from the effort of flexing his chest. "I'm going to catch it in my knapsack."

Miranda stared at Stanley in surprise. For as long as she had known him, he had always been the kind of boy who didn't like taking chances. Now, suddenly, he was like some brave new Stanley Nudelman.

And the new Stanley Nudelman puffed his chest out some more and leaped fearlessly over the barricade....

Unfortunately the new Stanley caught his foot on the table edge and landed with a faceplant on the other side. The knapsack slipped from his hands and the rest of the Widow's taffy skittered away across the floor.

He peeled his face up off the floor to see the teddy of terror inching toward him....

Stump!—scri-i-i-i-i-itch ... **Stump!—scri-i-i-i-i-itch** ... **Stump!—scri-i-i-i-i-itch** ...

And the new Stanley Nudelman did the only thing he could think of under the circumstances. He bravely squeezed his eyes shut and screamed like a baby:

"Waaaaaaaaaaahhhhhhhhhh—"

"—AAAAHHHHHHH—"

Stanley went on and on screaming as something was shaking him, and shaking him....

"—aaahhhhhunnnnhhh?"

Stanley peeked out with one eye. It wasn't Zombiekins shaking him, just Miranda.

Zombiekins, actually, had halted a few inches from Stanley's nose to nibble a piece of the Widow's taffy off the floor. Its fierce fangs made short work of the cement-like candy, devouring it

191

without a trace in seconds, and Stanley trembled at such a terrifying display of lethal power.

But instead of coming after Stanley when it had finished, Zombiekins just uttered a happy little moan, sat back on its teddy-bear haunches, and closed its eyes like a smiling baby. Then it appeared to go to sleep.

Laying there, still and sleeping, Zombiekins looked peaceful and not-at-all-bloodthirsty. As if it was nothing but a harmless stuffy after all—in spite of its somewhat macabre, half-dead appearance.

Miranda gave Stanley another shake and he looked up. All over the room, the other zombies had stopped advancing and were standing around, chewing intently. The Widow's taffy had halted them in their tracks!

Then something even more incredible happened. The first zombie began to twitch and jerk. . . . It shivered with strange convulsions . . . It bent forward, clutching its hands to its face . . .

. . . And when the zombie straightened up again, he was Sasha Govay, no more terrifying or undead than your average fourth grader.

Sasha stared around him with a blank, confused look, like someone waking from a deep sleep.

Behind his back, the other zombies had started twitching and jerking too. . . .

"W-what's happening?" Stanley asked, with a blank, confused look of his own.

"It was the taffy!" Miranda said. "You had the antidote in your knapsack all along, doofus!"

"How did you figure it out?" Stanley asked.

"I remembered what the Widow said when she gave it to you," Miranda explained. "'*You never know when it might come in handy….*'"

But any relief Stanley and Miranda might have felt at being spared from having their limbs ripped off by zombies didn't last long. Because as soon as the other kids had turned back to normal, they started asking questions. Very uncomfortable questions. Questions like "Where are we?" and "How did we get here?" and "Why does Bryce have a pair of scissors stuck in his chest?"

There was a heavy silence as everyone stared at the scissors jutting out of Bryce's chest. Talk about awkward.

Luckily, at just that moment, someone at the back yelled, "Teachers coming! Everybody hide!"

Kids scurried for cover like ants. Just as the last of them were squeezing into cupboards or behind curtains, Mr. Straap and Ms. Mellow appeared in the doorway.

But Stanley saw at once they weren't themselves: Mr. Straap staggered stiffly and awkwardly, with no more athletic coordination than an alligator on roller skates. And sweet-tempered Ms. Mellow gnashed her teeth and snarled with honey-toned strangled gurgling noises. . . .

As soon as the zombified teachers saw Stanley and Miranda, their eyes flashed with a fierce blood-thirsty gleam and they came drooling toward them like hungry wolves ... Zombie Ms. Mellow snarled sweetly ... Zombie Mr. Straap stumbled over a bump in the carpet....

Behind their backs, kids slipped from their hiding places and tiptoed out into the hall.

"We're dead!" Stanley squeaked.

"Relax," Miranda whispered. "We have the anti-dote, remember?"

She dangled two pieces of the Widow's taffy in front of her, and Mr. Straap and Ms. Mellow froze and sniffed the air like dogs.

"*Stayyyyyy*...." Miranda ordered. Ms. Mellow and Mr. Straap obeyed, ogling the taffy with tongues lolling out of their mouths.

Miranda tossed the taffy at their feet, and while the teachers pounced on the candy and devoured it like piranhas with a sweet tooth, she and Stanley ducked down behind an upturned table.

Within moments, the antidote started to take effect: The zombified teachers shivered, quivered, then popped back to normal.

Suddenly themselves again, Mr. Straap and Ms. Mellow stared around them in bewilderment at the wreckage of the staff room. For a moment, the two of them looked guilty as cornered criminals. Then, realizing they were alone, they relaxed a little, and a strange new look came over them. . . .

Mr. Straap gazed into Ms. Mellow's eyes and sighed, "Oh, Marsha!"

And Ms. Mellow goggled him back and whimpered, "Oh, Jacques!"

Then Mr. Straap swept Ms. Mellow up in his arms, and she hefted him in hers, and their lips met in a kiss.

Crouched behind their upturned table, Stanley and Miranda winced and averted their eyes.

"Ewwww!" Stanley shuddered. "Now *that* was scary."

STANLEY AND MIRANDA HAD NO TROUBLE SNEAKING
out of the staff room past Mr. Straap and Ms. Mellow.
But out in the halls, they soon discovered their
problems weren't over yet. In classroom after classroom, half the kids were still zombies—and in a few
minutes, school would be over and they would all
scatter to their homes.

"What can we do?" Stanley asked. "We'll never sneak the antidote to all these kids without getting caught."

And as long as there was one zombie left, it meant the whole plague could start all over again.

Fortunately, Miranda had a plan. She led Stanley down the stairwell to the playground door—the door where all the kids would exit at home time.

They didn't have to wait long. Almost as soon as the bell rang, the stairwell started to shake and rumble as if they were in the middle of an earthquake. Suddenly a stampede of children came barging, charging, rushing, racing, hustling, hurtling down the stairs, leaping three steps at a time, sliding down the handrails, shoving, jostling, dashing, darting, whooping, hollering, barreling, bounding, bustling, and finally bursting through the playground doors to freedom.

Just as suddenly, all the kids were gone and the stairwell fell silent.

Then came the zombies. A long procession, filing down the stairs in a slow, orderly manner. None of them hurrying, none of them yelling, none of them pushing or trying to budge each other in line.

At the sight of Stanley and Miranda, they growled and snarled and licked their zombie chops.

But Stanley and Miranda just lured them through the door and fed them taffy on the other side. A few minutes later, the playground was full of kids scratching their heads, and there wasn't a zombie in sight.

Walking home, Stanley and Miranda talked about what to do with Zombiekins.

"You have to give it back to the Widow," Miranda urged. "As long as you don't know what made it come to life, you never know when this zombie mayhem might start up all over again."

"I guess you're right," Stanley said glumly. "But I was really starting to like the little guy...."

He gazed fondly at Zombiekins. It was actually kind of cute—in a macabre, half-dead way.

Miranda was the one who noticed the wedge of cardboard sticking out of a shrub by the edge of the sidewalk.

"Hey, look," she said in surprise. "It's Zombiekins' box—and the instructions are still in it."

"Weird," Stanley said. "I'm sure I threw that in a trash can. How could it have gotten here?"

35

THE NEXT DAY AT SCHOOL, IT WAS AS IF NOTHING had happened. All the kids were back to normal again, except Felicity was off with a stomachache and Knuckles had developed a phobia of stuffed animals and dollies.

After school, Stanley hurried straight home. Fetch met him at the door, barking and tugging on Stanley's shirt in a panicky way.

"Hi, Stanley," Baby Rosalie called from the playroom. "Want to play tea party with me?"

But Stanley ignored them both and headed for his room. He had something he needed to do.

Fetch jumped in front of Stanley, barring his way, making desperate gestures and pointing down the hall toward the playroom. When Stanley reached to open his bedroom door, Fetch flung himself around Stanley's feet with a pleading yowl.

"Not now, boy," Stanley said. "I'm too busy to take you for a walk."

He pushed Fetch aside and opened the door.

Fetch hid whining and whimpering under the bed as Stanley unlocked his closet with a key from under his pillow, lifted a metal box down from the top shelf, then opened it with another key he shook out of his piggy bank.

Inside the metal box was another box, all covered over with tape. As Stanley lifted it out, Fetch let out 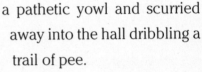 a pathetic yowl and scurried away into the hall dribbling a trail of pee.

Stanley was relieved to find Zombiekins still in its box. Of course, the instructions said it would remain a harmless stuffy as long as it wasn't exposed to direct moonlight—but Stanley was not the kind of boy who liked taking chances. He fingered the taffy hanging from a string around his neck as he locked Zombiekins back up in the metal box in his closet. On his way out of the room, he tripped over an empty box by his bed, but didn't think anything of it.

In the toy room down the hall, meanwhile, Rosalie was playing tea party with her favorite stuffies.

There was a chair for Benny the Dinosaur and another chair for his head. Whimsy was sitting in a pool of his own stuffing and Schlemmo, looking like he had been ripped apart and not-too-expertly put back together again, was propped up in a chair with ropes. While Rosalie pretended to pour the tea, one of Schlemmo's arms fell off and plopped onto his saucer.

"Bad Schlemmo!" Rosalie scolded. "Elbows off the table."

It was getting dark and the moon was climbing the sky outside the playroom window by the time Rosalie's mother finally called her to bed. After that, it wasn't long before Stanley and his family were all sound asleep—except for Fetch, who spent the night pacing the upstairs hall.

Outside, the night was still and the little town of Dementedyville was once again the quiet, uneventful place it always had been. The sort of place where nothing exciting or out of the ordinary ever happened. And now that Zombiekins was safely locked up in Stanley's closet, that was how it would probably stay.

Probably....

KEVIN

KEVIN BOLGER lives in Ottawa, Canada. He was an elementary school teacher for ten years before he published *Sir Fartsalot Hunts the Booger*. Naturally he always wanted to write a book where all the kids got turned into zombies. (Sweet revenge!) He previously collaborated with Aaron Blecha on the internet cartoon "Sir Fartsalot vs the Dragon," which can be seen at **www.sirfartsalot.com**.

AARON

AARON BLECHA was raised by a school of giant squids in Wisconsin and now lives with his wife in London, England. He works as an artist and animator, designing toys, making cartoons, and illustrating books, including the George Brown, Class Clown series. You can enjoy more of his twisted creations at **www.monstersquid.com**.

Thanks to Kristin Smith, Penguin book designer and honorary zombie, for her inspired page designs.

And to our editor, Jessica Rothenberg, for her infinite patience and unflagging support.

Like **Zombiekins**?
You won't want to miss

"*Don Quixote* for nine-year-olds, filtered through *Captain Underpants* and *Monty Python*. ... Entertaining and fun."
—*Quill and Quire*

"Amazingly well-written chapter book that balances the silly with the story.... A winner and surefire entertainer."
—*Young Adult (and Kids) Books Central*

"Kevin Bolger knows what young readers like. ... Just the book to make boys eager to turn the page."
—*Ottawa Citizen*